A SEAL'S PURPOSE

By Cora Seton

Author's Note

A SEAL's Consent is the fourth volume in the SEALs of Chance Creek series, set in the fictional town of Chance Creek, Montana. To find out more about Boone, Clay, Jericho and Walker, look for the rest of the books in the series, including:

A SEAL's Oath
A SEAL's Vow
A SEAL's Pledge
A SEAL's Consent
A SEAL's Resolve
A SEAL's Devotion
A SEAL's Desire
A SEAL's Struggle
A SEAL's Triumph

Also, don't miss Cora Seton's other Chance Creek series, the Cowboys of Chance Creek, the Heroes of Chance Creek, and the Brides of Chance Creek

The Cowboys of Chance Creek Series:

The Cowboy Inherits a Bride (Volume 0)
The Cowboy's E-Mail Order Bride (Volume 1)
The Cowboy Wins a Bride (Volume 2)
The Cowboy Imports a Bride (Volume 3)
The Cowgirl Ropes a Billionaire (Volume 4)
The Sheriff Catches a Bride (Volume 5)
The Cowboy Lassos a Bride (Volume 6)
The Cowboy Rescues a Bride (Volume 7)

The Cowboy Earns a Bride (Volume 8)
The Cowboy's Christmas Bride (Volume 9)

The Heroes of Chance Creek Series:

The Navy SEAL's E-Mail Order Bride (Volume 1)
The Soldier's E-Mail Order Bride (Volume 2)
The Marine's E-Mail Order Bride (Volume 3)
The Navy SEAL's Christmas Bride (Volume 4)
The Airman's E-Mail Order Bride (Volume 5)

The Brides of Chance Creek Series:

Issued to the Bride One Navy SEAL
Issued to the Bride One Airman
Issued to the Bride One Sniper
Issued to the Bride One Marine
Issued to the Bride One Soldier

The Turners v. Coopers Series:

The Cowboy's Secret Bride (Volume 1)
The Cowboy's Outlaw Bride (Volume 2)
The Cowboy's Hidden Bride (Volume 3)
The Cowboy's Stolen Bride (Volume 4)
The Cowboy's Forbidden Bride (Volume 5)

Visit Cora's website at www.coraseton.com
Find Cora on Facebook at facebook.com/CoraSeton
Sign up for my newsletter HERE.
www.coraseton.com/sign-up-for-my-newsletter

CHAPTER ONE

"IF I HAVE to marry a stranger in order to save the world, I'll do it," Kai Green told Boone Rudman as the sun broke over the horizon. "But I don't want Jericho's leavings. I want a woman who wants me."

The two men stood by a campfire near the bunkhouse that formed the headquarters of Base Camp, the sustainable community they were helping to build in Chance Creek, Montana, on an old ranch named Westfield. They both had served their country for years as Navy SEALs, but they couldn't be more different, Kai thought as he watched Boone consider his request. Boone's upright bearing and short clipped hair announced his military background wherever he went. Kai's blond hair had already grown until he once more looked like the California surfer he'd been growing up. Boone was just back from his morning run. Kai had already done his traditional 45-minute yoga routine, plus a half hour of meditation.

He'd almost got his head screwed back on after the unwelcome surprise he'd received the previous day.

Almost—but not quite.

It should have been a happy occasion—the wedding between his good friend Jericho Cook and Savannah Edwards, one of the women who helped run the Jane Austen–style bed-and-breakfast in the "manor" at the top of the hill—a large three-story stone building that looked straight out of Regency England. He'd been all set to celebrate—until he and the rest of the unmarried men had drawn straws to see who had to marry next.

And he'd pulled the short one.

Kai prided himself on the calm personality he'd worked so hard to attain. His adoptive family had practiced meditation every morning and night, and taught him and his sister to do so as well. It had been an antidote to the chaos of their younger years, and his ability to stay focused while everyone else was panicking had served him time and time again during his years as a Navy SEAL. It allowed him to see details others missed—and make good decisions about what to do next. It was what had held him together when his friends and family had protested his choice to join the military at age nineteen. Those had been difficult years, but he'd kept his course. Stayed true to who he was—and his need to protect those around him.

Back then he'd thought becoming a SEAL would confer on him a kind of superpower, one that would enable him to prevent suffering around the world. He was proud of his time in the service and of the missions he'd helped bring to fruition, but now he wanted something different. Not just to save others from suffering; but to prevent it in the first place. Base Camp was giving him that opportunity.

Still, the second he'd pulled that short straw, all that Zen serenity he'd worked for years to build came crashing down around his feet. He'd barely held his shit together during the ceremony and reception last night, struggling when the ever-present cameras focused on him. Kai and the others at Base Camp had made a devil's bargain with a billionaire named Martin Fulsom to be filmed night and day as part of the reality television show that documented their progress building their sustainable community, and there was nothing the show's director, Renata, liked better than to hound the poor schmuck whose turn it was next to take a trip to the altar.

She'd sure hounded him—all night long—until he'd finally gone to bed early just to get the cameras out of his face.

Marriage.

To someone he hadn't even met yet—

In the next forty days.

Now that it was his turn, he didn't think he could do it. Just thinking about it made his palms sweaty, his stomach tight. But he had to go through with it. There was no way out. If he didn't beat that deadline, Base Camp would be toast. And Base Camp was too important to lose. All around the world people struggled with food insecurity, and his new mission was to teach them how to make the most of whatever they had. He was participating in experiments with gardening techniques aimed at producing the most food for the least effort under all kinds of circumstances. More to the point, he was developing food preparation techniques that cut down on waste and used the least energy. He was building toward a future where he could share his message on his own cooking show.

And he was prepared to do whatever it took, he told himself sternly.

"Finding a bunch of new women for you to choose from is a waste of time," Boone said, bringing him back to the present. "I've got tons of eligible women who answered the wife wanted ad for Jericho. Why not just—"

"I said, I want someone who wants me." Kai winced. Now he sounded like an entitled teenager. He prided himself in taking what came his way, going with the flow—accepting what the Universe offered. Like his adopted parents had always told him—you could fight what life handed you, or you could take it and transform it into a future worth living. That philosophy had gotten him through all kinds of rough spots—even when the shit really hit the fan.

What was different now?

Why couldn't he see this twist of fate as just another step on the path to where he was meant to be? He'd been practicing acceptance for years, but today he was struggling to accept anything about this situation. He'd marry. He had to, or risk destroying everything he and his friends had worked so hard to build. But he didn't want Jericho's leavings. It was just good sense, he told himself. Those women had answered a call to marry Jericho, not him. Choosing one of them wouldn't work—the wavelength of her desire wouldn't match his.

Boone rubbed his stubbled jaw, but like a good leader, he kept his cool. Kai had no doubt the man wanted to throttle him. Boone was right; this was a total waste of time.

It was a stall tactic.

The truth was, Kai was panicking. He didn't trust the Universe to provide when it came to women. Or rather, he couldn't reconcile such a belief with his past experiences with them. When it came to women, he was—

What the hell was he?

Kai held out his hands over the flames in the fire pit. The nights were getting cool in Montana, and since many of Base Camp's residents still slept in tents, for the first time in months Boone had deemed it prudent to start a fire to warm everyone up that morning. Soon enough, hungry men and women would come looking for their breakfast. Kai needed to hop to it and get cooking, but he didn't feel much like hopping today.

When it came to women, he was—

Well, he had a bad habit of picking the wrong ones.

"If women were stray dogs," his adoptive mother, Wanda, had once remarked, "you'd be the guy choosing the crazy-ass mutt in the corner. The animal who refuses to come to the door of the cage to be pet. The one that bites you when you try to feed it."

At the time Kai had thought she was being unfair,

but he was older now. Wiser.

And he knew she was right.

There'd been Kelsie, the one who sold pinecone collages at the local swap meet and lived with a family of gypsies in Cerritos. There'd been Holly, the exotic dancer he'd convinced himself was ready to settle down. There'd been Rachel, who wrote post-feminist poetry under the nom-de-plume Guerrilla Pistol. And India, who'd decided to become a superhero for cats and paced the dark underbelly of Long Beach at night in a tabby-colored leotard and cape, collecting strays until her family had her admitted to a cushy hospital for a good long rest.

All interesting in their own way, but as his mother pointed out—

"Far too skinny. Far too insubstantial. Far more interested in navel-gazing than in you. Kai," she'd added, with more than a touch of exasperation. "Do you think you chase these women because they remind you of your mother?"

"You're my mother."

"You know what I mean."

She was probably right, Kai had to admit. His birth mother, whom he hadn't seen since he was seven, had been as fly-by-night as the women he'd dated. What did that say about his intelligence? He kept finding new people to leave him high and dry, when he'd been saved from that pain by the Ledbetters.

"All right. Fine. What do you want in your ad? Describe your perfect woman," Boone said, cutting into his thoughts again.

What did he want? An image popped into his head. The kind of image that always got him into trouble. A barefoot, waifish, gypsy-clothed, elfin-faced wild child with a tortured past and an intriguing way of making it through the world.

"Sensible," he said out loud.

Boone raised an eyebrow. "Sensible?"

Kai pictured Kelsie—the way she drifted from idea to idea. "Grounded."

"O-kay," Boone drawled. He pulled out his phone and started tapping the keys.

Kai thought about Holly, who was late to almost everything—including the job where she took off her clothes. "Competent."

Boone kept tapping, and Kai thought about Rachel's bitter, acid observations about life and love—and the people around them. "Optimistic."

He thought about India and her superhero costume. "Sane," he added. Although he had to admit, he had a soft spot for stray animals, too. In fact, wanting to save cats wasn't all that odd if you asked—

"Looking for a sensible, grounded, competent, optimistic, sane woman for a lifetime commitment," Boone read back.

"That ought to do it." But Kai was cringing. *Accept what life brings you*, he reminded himself. It was the only way.

"I'll just polish that up and submit it to some dating sites. Renata will make sure to show it during the next episode, too," Boone told him.

"I'll get breakfast going." Kai was grateful to escape to his kitchen, off to one side of the bunkhouse's main room. When it came to food, he knew exactly what he was doing. In fact, he had it down to a science.

"Save me some coffee," Boone called as he headed for his desk.

"Will do." *Find me the right wife*, he wanted to add but didn't.

Even Boone couldn't pull that off.

Back in his kitchen, Kai tried to get himself together. At least here he was in control. He had his ingredients, his appliances, and the knowledge he'd gathered through years of study and practice. Throw him scraps, and he'd transform them into a feast.

As he chopped and diced fresh ingredients for an omelet, Kai found a semblance of calm. The sky outside was brightening by the moment. A new day was a new beginning, and maybe Boone would surprise him and actually find a woman who—

Angus McBride burst into the kitchen and shut the door behind him with a click, turning the old-fashioned key in the lock. He was a large man with red hair and hazel eyes. Normally cheerful, he'd been quiet since his girlfriend, Win Lisle, had left Base Camp to return home a few weeks ago.

Kai stopped what he was doing. He'd forgotten the kitchen even had a door; they never closed it, let alone used the lock.

"We've got a problem," Angus said. "A big one."

Kai had never seen the man so upset, except when Win had left. "What problem?" He tried to recapture a little of the calm he'd felt just moments ago, but it was like grasping at smoke.

"The root cellar. It's..." Angus threw his hands up in a defeated gesture. "It's... empty."

"Empty? What do you mean, empty?" Kai dropped his knife onto the cutting board and wiped his hands on his apron. Without those food stores, they were in trouble. The reality television show Martin Fulsom had forced them to participate in included a series of difficult tasks they needed to accomplish in order to keep their land. One of them was to produce all the food they needed over the winter. Since they'd only started last spring, he'd given them a grace period during which they could purchase food, but that grace period was over as of the beginning of October. Fulsom had allowed them to stock up on coffee, chocolate, salt and pepper. Otherwise they were on their own. They had a huge vegetable garden, two heated greenhouses in which they would grow greens over the winter, several old fruit trees someone had planted on the ranch years ago, chickens, pigs, several beehives, a field of wheat, a herd of bison and a milk cow.

Kai had been so proud of the progress they'd made toward producing their own food. Their meals would be plain over the next seven months, but filling and delicious nonetheless. They had plenty of honey stored up for sweetener, and while they hadn't harvested and ground their wheat, they'd picked bushels of starchy vegetables for the interim. He wouldn't be able to make any more breakfast burritos until they had flour again, but he could still fry up a mess of potatoes and keep his people happy.

One of his triumphs had been the cheeses he'd produced. He'd learned to make mozzarella-style and other soft cheeses that took little time to prepare—and cheddar varieties that would need to cure for months, but that they'd enjoy next year. He'd learned to churn butter, a daily chore that was time-consuming and took more skill than he'd expected. One by one, he'd learned to make most things he needed from scratch.

Still, without those vegetables they'd harvested and stored in the root cellar, their meals were going to be nothing but meat, eggs and cheese, whatever greens they could grow in the dead of winter... and an apple now and then.

Angus shushed him. "We can't let anyone else know. Definitely not Renata."

Kai scrubbed a hand over his jaw. Thank goodness they weren't being filmed right now; Renata had so much footage of him cooking she'd stopped sending cameras into the kitchen. "What happened?" he asked in a lower tone, struggling to calm himself again. There was a way out of this. All he had to do was listen, think things over and make rational decisions.

"Someone must have broken in. I'm not kidding, Kai. It's all gone. Every last potato."

Kai knew why he was emphasizing potatoes. Until they could harvest the wheat and make flour, they'd be low on carbohydrates without potatoes, winter squashes and other root vegetables. That's why they'd planted so many of them. If they were all gone...

"That's a hell of a lot of food. How could someone get it without our seeing?"

Angus shrugged. "They must have come at night. The cellar isn't locked. It's far enough away from the houses that someone could sneak in if they were quiet. We never thought to guard it. We keep making that mistake; thinking there's safety in numbers or that we're not in danger because we're home in the United States rather than abroad in some war zone."

Kai knew what he meant; a stalker had already penetrated their encampment once and nearly killed Nora, Clay Pickett's wife.

"Hell." Kai thought fast, but he could barely process the information. Someone had stolen their entire harvest? Bushels and bushels of potatoes, onions, carrots and more? That would take a lot of people a lot of time.

"Could someone really get a truck near the root cellar without us hearing?"

"They must have," Angus said. "It's the only explanation."

"During the wedding," Kai said, comprehension dawning on him. "They waited until all of us were up at the manor. When was the last time someone checked the stores?" He hadn't been in the root cellar for several days. He was still making use of fresh produce right out of the garden, although that would need to change soon.

He shook his head, the magnitude of the loss washing over him again.

"As far as I can figure it's been two days. Last week we focused on harvesting. Since then we've been working on the greenhouses and the hydroponics setup."

"Whoever it was has been watching us. They knew where we'd be yesterday."

"Who the hell could it be?"

Kai counted his breaths in and out, trying once more to settle his thoughts. "Montague. Who else? He wants this land, right? Maybe he's not above playing dirty to get it." The developer was part of the reality show, too. The bad guy waiting in the wings to steal their land if they didn't reach all their goals. He already had plans drawn up for a subdivision of seventy homes he wanted to build on this property, and Martin Fulsom had pledged to hand Westfield over to him if Kai and the others didn't meet the requirements on the reality television show.

Kai hated to think about a housing development swallowing this beautiful ranch.

"You really think Fulsom would let him have it?" Angus asked.

Kai regarded him in surprise. "You think he wouldn't?"

Angus looked away. "I guess I hoped that a man supposedly dedicated to furthering sustainable living wouldn't play fast and loose with a bit of heaven like Westfield. That maybe it was all a gimmick, and no matter what, he wouldn't let it be developed."

"He can't go back on his word. If the show ends, we lose and this land isn't developed, no one would ever take him seriously again," Kai pointed out.

"Then this contest just got ugly," Angus said. "We're being filmed; Montague's people aren't. They can keep picking off our resources any time they want to."

"Unless we get more serious about security. We've got to tell Boone."

Angus nodded. "You know, I wouldn't put it past Renata to do something along these lines to make the show more interesting."

Kai thought that over. "You're right, but I don't think it's her this time. If she pulls something like this, it will be near the end, when it doesn't matter so much if we catch her at it. If she tried it now, and we found out, the show would go off the rails."

"Yeah, I guess."

"We increase security. And then what? We need more greens—and starchy foods. How much can we grow in the greenhouses?"

"I don't know. We might be fucked."

Kai refused to believe it. "We've still got food," he pointed out. "They didn't steal our bison herd, right? We've got lots of meat. Plenty of people have survived with less."

He and his sister Grace certainly had.

Kai shook that thought away. "We already planned to harvest a bison this fall," he went on. "We've got chickens and pigs, so we'll have eggs and pork. We've got whatever we can grow in the greenhouses through the remainder of the fall and winter—"

"Which none of us has ever done before," Angus said.

"We'll figure it out." They'd have to. Kai knew why Angus was worried, though. It was one thing to build a greenhouse, and another thing altogether to manage succession growing in a way that kept the correct amount of food coming to the table. The seedlings they'd managed to grow hydroponically were struggling so far. Kai, Angus, Boone and Samantha Wentworth, the other member of the team devoted to growing their food, had been trying to get the nutrient mix right for the indoor plants. It was still an imperfect science for them.

Plus, the greenhouses were vulnerable. The main one had already been destroyed once. A heavy snowfall or a high wind could destroy it again. Or a man like Montague. Then what?

"We'll have to plant more potatoes. Inside." Kai could easily interpret the look Angus sent him. Neither of them knew if that was possible. It should work, but—

"We'd better plant them today," Angus said. "It'll be months before they're ready. What do we do until then?"

"There are still carrots in the garden, cabbages and some potatoes, right?"

"Some."

"I'll do an inventory today and figure out a plan to stretch them out. Meanwhile we need a lock on the root cellar."

"I'm on it," Angus said. "We'd better post a guard there at night, too."

"How do we let people know what's going on without letting Renata in on our secret?"

"We can't hold a meeting," Angus mused. "We'll have to pass the information on to people one at a time."

"If it is Montague or Renata who stole the vegetables, then we'll need to watch everything at night—the bison herd, the chickens and pigs… There are only ten of us men," Kai said. "If half of us are up all night, that means we'll need more sleep during the day. Renata's going to notice."

"We'll figure it out. Meanwhile, you can distract her."

"Me? How?"

"You're next up for getting married. Keep the drama high. Keep her focused on you, not the patrols. Or the root cellar. Okay?"

"Okay," Kai said reluctantly. High drama?

Wasn't he supposed to look for the opposite of that when he chose a wife?

"WHAT'S THIS?"

"Nothing!" Addison Reynolds snatched the paperback out of her sister Felicity's hands and shoved it back into her faux-leather oversize purse. She'd been rummaging around for her water bottle to refill before she accompanied Felicity to sunrise yoga. She'd arrived in Manhattan late last night, but that hadn't stopped Felicity from waking her up at 5:00 a.m. Addison lived miles away in Hartford, Connecticut, but she traveled to New York City every chance she got and camped out in Felicity's fabulous guest room. The price she paid was being at the mercy of her sister's constant campaign to improve her life.

"*The Freedom of Yes?* You're actually reading that book?"

"It's for my book club," Addison lied, wishing she'd never dumped out the contents of her damn bag on the impeccable kitchen counter of her sister's penthouse. As usual, ever since she'd arrived, the more Felicity flitted around like a gorgeous butterfly, the more she careened around like a drunken moth. It wasn't fair the way Felicity glided through life like she'd been given some secret elixir of knowledge at birth. How did she manage to always look perfect, be perfect, do the perfect thing at the perfect moment? The fact that she was younger than Addison only made it worse.

But that was nothing new. Felicity had been out-shining her since she was three years old.

"You're not in a book club." Felicity grabbed for the book again. Addison snatched her purse away, glad for the distraction. She refused to let her memories drive a wedge between her and her sister. She'd accepted the reality of their situation. Felicity was beautiful, and she was merely pretty. And Felicity's kind of beauty lifted her high above anything Addison could attain.

"How do you know?"

"I know everything about you. Besides, you work all the time. When would you read books?" Felicity grabbed for the paperback again and this time succeeded in pulling it free. "I can't believe you're reading this."

"Why not?" Addison read books—as often as she could. She lived vicariously through other people's adventures. She couldn't help that she hadn't been handed an exciting modeling career like Felicity had.

Or a husband worth millions.

Addison stuffed down her jealousy and tried—unsuccessfully—to pull the paperback out of Felicity's hands.

"For one thing, you never say yes to anything." Felicity turned the book over and began to read the blurb on the back. "'Worried? Stressed? Driven to distraction by your to-do list? What if you've got it all wrong? I'm here to tell you that you don't have to work so hard.' Hmm, I think this woman's on to something, Addison." Felicity read on. "'Just say yes to the universe and see what adventures unfold.'" Felicity lowered the book and fixed her green eyes on Addison. The same green eyes that had helped win her first beauty pageant at three, her first modeling gig at five and left her at the top of her career at twenty-six. "Are you actually thinking about trying this?"

"Of course not." Addison snatched the book back. It had been stupid of her to ever pick it up. It had caught her eye in the window of the bookstore she passed every day on her way to work at Kelson, Kelson and Klein back in Connecticut, and the ridiculous premise of its title worked on her until she finally had to go in and see what it was all about.

It sounded lovely letting the universe decide your fate—until you realized what a crap job it did most of the time. Halfway through with the book, Addison was carrying it around only until she passed a thrift shop, although donating it was probably cruel. It would only fall into the hands of someone more gullible than she was.

"No, of course not," Felicity echoed, "because God forbid you let anything happen by chance. What was it your last boyfriend called you?"

"I don't want to talk about it." She was sick and tired of having endless variations of this same conversation with her sister.

Felicity came and went like a will 'o wisp on the wind. If she had an impulse, she followed it. If a thought crossed her mind, she expressed it. That was all well and good if you were five foot ten and weighed 114 pounds—and had inherited their mother's luminous skin and emerald-green eyes. And had been cosseted and fussed over by that same mother since you took your first steps down the beauty pageant catwalk. Unfortunately, Addison took after her father—brown hair, gray eyes and an unremarkable body.

Unlike Felicity, she had to work for her living—

Well, that wasn't exactly fair. Felicity worked, too—often under uncomfortable circumstances, and she was constantly watching her weight, while Addison could grab an ice cream sundae now and then without being afraid she'd lose her actuarial job at the insurance company.

As for Felicity's relationship with their mother… Addison wasn't sure whether to envy it or run away screaming. Marjorie Reynolds had peaked at sixteen, when she won the Miss Connecticut pageant, and had never succeeded in making the leap to a modeling career. She was a force to be reckoned with in Felicity's life. Determined to take part in every minute of her daughter's success.

Addison had experienced her mother's intense focus once upon a time, when it had been her on that beauty pageant stage—before Felicity was old enough to compete in the bigger pageants. It had been a heady time. She still remembered the rush of fear and excitement when she'd stepped out before the judges. She'd loved to perform. Had won a competition or two. When she received a crown, her mother's love was as sweet as cotton candy. When she lost—

Well.

That was long past. No sense worrying about it now.

She worried about Felicity, though. Still caught up in the game—

But Felicity was always a winner. And when Addison looked out at the skyline from Felicity's penthouse, she had a hard time keeping her jealousy under control. She wanted this. The view, the beautiful furniture and appliances. The Manhattan address... And not just the beautiful trappings. She wanted to feel like Felicity felt. Like she was someone who mattered.

"I want to talk about it." Felicity snatched the book out of her hand again. "You're twenty-nine. Single."

"Thank you for reminding me."

"Beautiful and talented—and wasting your life playing it safe. Isn't it time you took a chance?" She waved the book in Felicity's face. "Say yes."

"I don't want to say yes." She'd long since learned smart choices and hard work were the way to get ahead for someone like her.

"Uptight. That's what Kevin called you when he dumped you. Uptight. Rigid. A twenty-nine-year-old stick in the mud."

"Why are you being so mean?" Sometimes Addison felt that her sister's life was so unerringly successful she jumped on Addison's failures because she got bored.

"Because its true!" Felicity exploded. "All you do is go to that damn job and work overtime."

"So I can save up for a down payment—"

"In New Jersey, which is as close to the City as you'll ever be able to afford to buy a house. And where you'll be bored for the rest of your life, like you are in Connecticut. You could rent a place here."

"I could rent a closet here," Addison corrected her. "I'm not going to live in New Jersey. I have lots of fun. When I'm not working, I go to parties all the time."

"You *throw* parties all the time, you mean."

"What's the difference?" Addison loved to throw

parties. Had since she was a teenager. It was like being onstage in a way—like throwing a performance for your guests in which they could participate rather than sitting in the audience. "You should have come to the last one. You would have loved it. The theme was—"

"The theme was, the theme was, the theme was—when are you going to stop playacting at life and start living it? Have you ever realized you always throw parties for someone else and you never celebrate yourself?"

Stung, Addison turned away. Her parties were the best part of her life, and everyone said they were wonderful. So inventive. Always something new. What was wrong with that? If she couldn't afford to go everywhere and do everything, she recreated it as best she could in her little apartment in Hartford. She didn't need to be the center of attention. Not like Felicity. She loved celebrating her friends. None of them were rich, either. They appreciated the way she brought some glamour to their lives. It might be different if she was living in the City, but New York was so expensive she'd never be able to own her own—

"Addy, what do you want more than anything?" Felicity demanded.

"Your penthouse," Addison said without thinking, then bit her lip. Shit. The last thing she wanted was for Felicity to know how much she envied her. "I mean—" She was going to say she wanted to open her own event planning business, but that was a secret she'd held close for years, and she found she couldn't voice it. Somehow

Felicity's penthouse encompassed that desire: it had been Felicity's reward for achieving her modeling goals. Addison wanted to achieve her goals, too.

Felicity blinked. "Done," she said after a beat.

"Yeah, right." She wasn't anywhere near close to becoming an event planner, certainly not in New York City. She didn't deserve a place like Felicity's penthouse, and even if she did—

"No, I'm serious. I invited you here this weekend to tell you something." Felicity took a breath. "It's kind of big, Addy. Please don't throw a wobbly."

"You're scaring me," Addison said. "What is it?"

"Evan and I are moving to Rome. It makes sense for my career, and his company is opening up a division there, and—"

"Rome?" Addison gripped the counter when the floor seemed to drop out from under her. "You're moving to Rome?"

Figured.

Another adventure for Felicity. More same old, same old for her. She pictured her drive back to Connecticut Sunday night, imagining all the fun and excitement Felicity would have in her new life. Meanwhile, her existence would become that much narrower. No more trips to New York with free accommodations at Felicity's place. No more riding the coattails of Felicity's glamorous life.

"Addison, did you hear me?"

She made herself smile. "Of course. That's amazing for you, sweetie. I'll come visit, and you'll show me all around."

"You weren't paying attention."

Addison tried to play back the conversation in her mind. "Your career. Evan's company."

"Mom," Felicity said quietly.

"What about Mom?"

"She won't be there."

Addison's breath caught in her throat as the implications became clear to her. Felicity was making a break for it.

"Oh, Felicity."

Her sister put up a hand. "I don't want to talk about it. Evan's insisting. I know he's right, but… it isn't easy. She's going to be so angry."

Addison could only nod. Her mother would be furious at Felicity's defection.

"It's just… she keeps saying…"

Addison moved to hug her when Felicity's eyes filled with tears. "It's okay."

"No, it's not." Felicity broke free and wiped the back of her arm over her cheeks. "She keeps talking about the end of my career. How I'd better live it up now because it's all almost over for me."

"Jesus." Addison wanted to throttle her mother. "You know that's not true."

"Sure, it is. I'm twenty-six. She's right; I won't be a model forever. I need to figure out what comes next— before I'm forced to. I can't do that with her around."

"Evan's pretty smart to bring you somewhere you can have space to do that," Addison admitted. "I'm going to miss you, though."

"No, you're not." Felicity lifted her chin and forced a smile to her face. "Because you're going to be too busy having your own adventure."

"Right. An actuarial adventure. In Connecticut. Whoop-de-doo!"

"Not an actuarial adventure," Felicity corrected. "A crazy, wonderful, New York City adventure. I'm giving you my penthouse." She braced Addison's shoulders with her hands. "I want you to take it."

Addison stilled. Was she for real?

"If—and only if—you do this," Felicity added, reaching for *The Freedom of Yes* and shaking it at Addison.

"What do you mean?"

"I mean you have to say yes—to everything—for one month. If you do, I'll give you my penthouse mortgage-free for one year."

"Evan won't—"

"Evan will throw in the property taxes. He does whatever I tell him." Felicity held her gaze. "You know it's true. Come on. Take this chance, Addy. Do it."

Evan did do everything Felicity asked him, but this was crazy. "What do you mean say yes to everything?"

"I mean say yes to everything." Felicity smiled her trademark devilish smile, the one she'd had since grade school.

Addison thought fast. That was far too open-ended. She was liable to get hurt. "There would have to be some ground rules. What if someone asks me to kill someone. Or smuggle drugs?"

"You don't have to kill anyone. Or smuggle drugs. Or drive drunk. Or have unprotected sex—or sex with anyone you don't want to, for that matter."

"But—"

"Addison, are you going to say yes to this chance to live here, at the top of the world, in Manhattan? Your favorite place in the universe? Or are you going to say no, crawl back to your safe little hole and hate yourself forever?"

Damn it, her sister knew all her buttons. She'd learned from the best. Addison took a deep breath and hoped like hell she wouldn't regret this.

"Yes."

KAI PULLED CONTAINERS of vegetables he'd presliced last night out of the refrigerator and put them on the counter. He'd halved the amount of greens he'd normally add to the omelet, conscious of how far he needed to make them go. He'd added a few extra eggs to make up for it. They had eggs in spades, thanks to their flock of chickens. The sun was far too low on this late fall morning to cook with the solar ovens he liked to use, so the key to making this meal as sustainable as possible was to keep the cooking time to a minimum. That meant veggies sliced razor thin, a single burner heated until the butter he bought locally sizzled when dropped in and then a quick sauté of the vegetables, followed by the pour of the eggs collected minutes ago from the community's free-range chickens. Swirl the pan around.

Let the eggs set. Add some shredded homemade cheese, fold them over and voilà, a huge omelet to be shared among several of the inhabitants of Base Camp.

He looked at the potatoes already frying in a second pan. Nothing to do but serve them now.

The loss of the root cellar hit him all over again.

There was nothing he could do about it right now, though, so to distract himself, Kai focused on his long-term goal. He kept cooking, and even though the cameras weren't around, he acted as if every motion he made was being scrutinized by people all over the country.

Kai had a plan—and it didn't involve obscurity. He was a SEAL who liked to make meals. There was a cooking show title in there somewhere, and he was going to find it—and find a producer interested in making him a star. Not because he was high on himself. Because he was high on teaching people about what he was doing—sustainable cooking. Sustainable food preparation. Sustainable feasts. And learning how to balance food, gardening and cash flow to make sure your family never went hungry, no matter what your circumstances.

He had already made some moves in the direction of securing his own show, but first he had to make sure Base Camp survived. He'd given his word to Boone and the others to see this through, and he meant to keep it—despite disasters like stolen food.

When the meal was ready, Kai brought it to a folding table in the main room, where he laid it out buffet-style. He ducked back into the kitchen and brought out homemade salsa as an accompaniment, and soon he was dishing out food to a line of hungry men and women. There were fifteen of them now that Win had taken off for California; ten men and five women. Four couples had already married, which meant six more to go before they met the conditions set by Fulsom.

Now it was his turn.

The loss of their food stores had knocked that little detail out of his mind for the last half hour, but as everyone left the bunkhouse to sit around the campfire to eat, Kai couldn't help thinking about it.

What would it be like to marry a woman and commit to making their relationship last forever? Could he handle that?

Kai wasn't sure.

He returned to the kitchen, made some notations about the meal in the thick notebook he kept full of recipes and ideas, loaded up his own plate and headed outside, hoping to forget his troubles for a few minutes, but as soon as he sat down on one of the logs around the fire, Nora, a serious woman with dark brown hair and eyes, leaned forward and said, "I heard Boone's finding you a wife."

Instantly, one of the camera men filming the proceedings edged closer, and Kai wondered if Nora had been prompted to ask him that. Sometimes Renata liked to push the show in a certain direction, especially when it came to the next man who had to marry.

He took in the smile quirking Nora's lips and bit

back a groan. If Nora thought the situation was funny, he was doomed. "That's right."

"You shouldn't sound like a man who's on his way to his own funeral," Harris Wentworth said. A sniper, he'd recently married Samantha, who'd originally come to marry Curtis but had fallen for Harris instead. "Boone's good at finding women."

"He'd better be. He's got my future in his hands," Kai said sourly.

"I know what I'm doing," Boone said complacently from where he sat on a log next to his wife, Riley.

"He does," Riley agreed. "Although I'm probably biased."

"Have you put up Kai's ad yet, Boone?" Avery asked. A petite redhead, Avery had made it clear she meant to pursue a film career. She liked to act, but she also took turns behind the camera when she could and was busy writing a screenplay.

"Thinking of answering it?" Clay teased. Another Navy SEAL, Clay had married Nora after killing her stalker. He and Nora stuck close together most of the time. Kai wondered if he'd ever have a relationship like that.

"No," Avery said shortly. "No offense, Kai."

"None taken." Kai was ready to go back inside. He knew what Avery meant—she had an unmistakable crush on Walker Norton, the large Native American man eating his breakfast several feet away. He knew, too, that Walker had heard every word she'd said, even if he hadn't reacted. And that the SEAL would be pissed if Avery did answer the ad. Those two needed to stop mooning over each other and get together, for everyone's sake.

"What kind of woman are you after?" Angus asked. "Let me guess; a gymnast." Kai wondered how he could joke after their conversation in the kitchen, then decided the man wanted Renata focused on Kai's impending marriage, like he'd said before.

"I bet he asked for a prep cook," Nora said.

"Or a sous chef, maybe," Riley hazarded.

"He asked for someone sensible," Boone told them.

Hoots of laughter came from all around.

"Sensible?" Curtis Lloyd said. A big, burly man, he was still single, too, after Harris had stolen his bride, but he didn't seem as bitter about it as he once had been. "Man, someone needs to have a talk with you, Kai."

"I might have doctored up his ad a little bit," Boone admitted. "Made it a little more interesting."

"Good," Angus pronounced, then fell silent when everyone turned to look at him. "Uh… I mean… interesting how?"

"You'll have to wait and see."

Kai didn't like the sound of that.

When his phone buzzed in his pocket, he got up and returned to the bunkhouse gratefully. It was Grace, his biological sister, who lived in Long Beach near their adopted family and worked for Child Protective Services.

"Hey," he said when he accepted the call.

"Hey, yourself. It's your turn, huh? Going to get

hitched?"

He'd texted her about drawing the short straw. "Going to try."

"Kai—do you think this is a good idea?"

He knew why she was asking. His track record with women wasn't great, and they'd long ago promised themselves that when they got serious about a partner, they'd make sure they were with the right person before marrying. Their biological mother had made no commitments at all to anyone. Neither of them wanted to inflict that kind of mayhem on the world.

"I have to try. It was part of the deal to join Base Camp."

"I thought you'd find someone before your turn came up."

"This is a pretty small place, and I've been pretty busy. I haven't had that many chances to meet a woman."

"So now what? Boone finds you one? Like he did for Harris?"

It was a little strange to know his family watched *Base Camp* so closely. Kai tried not to think about it most of the time. "Yeah," he said shortly. There wasn't any point in pretending otherwise.

"Maybe he'll be better at it than you are," she mused.

Kai laughed. "He couldn't be worse, I guess."

"Take care of yourself, though. I don't want to see you get hurt."

"I know." Neither of them needed any more pain in

their lives. "What about you? How are things with Tom?" Her sister had been dating a police officer for nearly six months. Something of a record for her, too. She got so wrapped up in her work, her boyfriends often felt neglected, but Tom seemed something of a workaholic, too.

"Good. Really good." She hesitated. "Kai—we got engaged yesterday."

"Wow." He hadn't expected that, and his stomach did a kind of flip. He was as protective of Grace's happiness as she was of his. "Congratulations." He began to stack up dishes and utensils near the sink to prepare for the washing up when the meal was done.

"Thanks. We'll have a nice long engagement," she added. "We're thinking about next June for the wedding."

"That's really great." Kai tried to take it in. His little sister—married. "I mean it, Grace. I'm happy for you."

"Find someone good. I want you to have your person, too."

"Is that what Tom is? Your person?" He turned on the faucet and ran a sinkful of soapy water.

"Yeah, I think so."

Grace sounded happy, and something shifted in Kai's chest. It was like he'd been holding his breath for a long time and the air had whooshed out of his lungs, creating space to take a new breath. Grace could be all right.

Maybe he could, too.

"I've got to go," she said. "But keep me updated. I

want to know what happens."

"You can always watch the episode next week."

"Jerk."

Kai laughed. "I'll keep you updated."

"Good." Grace cut the call, and Kai looked at the dishes waiting to be washed, happy to have a minute alone. Maybe things were changing in his life. If Grace could find a husband, why couldn't he find a wife?

Kai supposed he'd have to wait and see if anyone answered Boone's ad.

"ARE YOU SERIOUS? Ombre hair dye? Is that still a thing?" Addison asked as they sat in the waiting area of a very expensive salon.

"Yes, it's still a thing," Felicity said. "And you would look fabulous with it. Silver-white from the roots down, fading out to your natural color. With your eyes, you'll look otherworldly."

The stylist, who was sweeping up from her last customer, nodded her agreement.

"I don't want to look otherworldly. I work for an insurance company."

"Do you want my penthouse or not?"

"Yes." Addison bit back a groan. All morning, Felicity had been torturing her. Making her try hot yoga, a chia smoothie that nearly made her vomit, a manicure with sparkly nails.

Now she was going to butcher her hair.

It was worth it for a shot at Felicity's penthouse, though. She'd have to change jobs anyway if she moved

A SEAL'S PURPOSE | 33

here, and she'd re-dye her hair and ditch the nails as soon as she was out of Felicity's sight. She figured Felicity wouldn't be able to do much from Rome.

Addison squirmed through the hair appointment, doing her best to keep up with Felicity and the stylist's chatter, dreading the outcome. Usually she regarded her trips to the salon as a welcome reprieve from her busy life. When she could, she went with Felicity, who made everything fun and sometimes sprung for expensive treatments Addison wouldn't buy otherwise. Addison felt guilty about accepting them, but the difference in their bank accounts meant sometimes she had to accept charity or never get to do anything Felicity liked to do. Besides, when she managed to escape their mother's hovering, Felicity liked to hover herself. Addison let her, understanding the impulse.

"Take a look," the stylist finally said after what seemed like hours of fuss and bother.

Addison cringed, hoping it wasn't too awful. But when the stylist turned her around in the chair and showed her the result, she was pleasantly surprised. Felicity was right—she looked... different.

Like the kind of woman things happen to.

Addison bent nearer the mirror to get a better look. It was like she'd taken on a whole new identity in the last few hours, and the idea appealed to her in a way she wouldn't have guessed. She'd thought she'd come to grips with her role in her family and in the world.

Maybe she hadn't.

Catching Felicity's gaze in the mirror, Addison repressed a twist of sadness. She was going to miss her sister so much.

She closed her eyes at the thought of it.

"Addison?"

Focus on the present, Addison instructed herself. It wouldn't do to get teary now. Her sister needed space to find her way. She was grateful to Evan for realizing that and encouraging her to move to Europe.

If only it wasn't so far away.

But that was the whole point, wasn't it?

"It's great," she said, waving off Felicity's concern. She couldn't let her sister know how much this was affecting her.

After all, she'd get to enjoy her new penthouse. If she could change where she lived, maybe she could change who she was, too. She'd be starting over. New town, new home, new job.

She didn't have to be boring old Addison anymore.

"Let's see: hair, nails, breakfast. What's next?" Felicity considered her. "Clothes."

"Felicity—" Dollar signs racked up in her mind. Felicity had already spent a small fortune on her, and despite how exciting it felt to think about changing herself when she moved, she knew that wasn't really possible. She'd still be Addison. Still be an actuary.

Still be boring.

"Was that a no?"

"No. I mean—yes, clothes. But I can't afford them."

"I can."

"You've spent too much—"

"Yes or no?"

Evan was going to have a heart attack when he saw this month's bills, but with what the two of them earned, maybe it wasn't any big deal. Besides, she knew that look in Felicity's eyes. She wasn't going to give up until she got her way.

"Yes."

By the end of the day, Addison was exhausted. Felicity hadn't bought her a couple of new items; she'd insisted on purchasing Addison a whole new wardrobe and made her promise to wear her new clothes for the rest of the month. In fact, she'd forced Addison to keep on one of the outfits for the rest of the day. She kept dragging her around to shops owned by friends, showing Addison off in a way she'd never done before. The friends seemed to find her intriguing, a heady experience for someone who usually got ignored at the parties she sometimes attended with her sister.

Maybe this month was exactly what she needed. A chance to try something new. To break out of the mold. Have a few adventures.

If it didn't take, she'd go back to her usual way of being.

She still needed to make sensible choices or spend the rest of her life broke.

"Live a little," Felicity kept telling her. "Have you been paying attention to all the people I've introduced you to today? They're not waiting to pursue their dreams."

Maybe not; but they weren't necessarily getting ahead, either. Most of the little boutiques they'd been to probably had razor-thin profit margins, Addison thought. Most of them would be gone in a few years. Where would that leave their owners?

Back at the penthouse, take-out containers in hand from a darling little Eritrean restaurant Felicity insisted she try, Addison collapsed into one of her sister's beautiful leather chairs and flipped on the television.

Base Camp. One of her favorite reality television shows. She could happily watch that for the next hour. A bunch of crazy Navy SEALs and women running around in Jane Austen gowns. What wasn't to like?

Felicity came in with two plates and passed one to Addison. "I was thinking. After dinner we could go—"

"Oh my god, give me a break," Addison cried. "I've said yes a million times. I need to r—"

"Shh!" Felicity hissed, her gaze arrested by the television screen, where the show had blinked off and an ad popped up. It showed the face of one of *Base Camp*'s stars—a handsome Navy SEAL with bleach-blond hair and a square jaw.

"It's Kai—the cute surfer!" Felicity watched the show as assiduously as Addison did.

Bold block letters across the photograph on the screen read, "Wife Wanted."

Felicity smiled. "Well, would you look at that."

Addison's heart flipped. She'd marry Kai in a second. He was so handsome. As buff as a bodybuilder, broad-shouldered and blond. And he was a man who cared so deeply about what he did; he cooked like an artist creating art—like the masters at the Cordon Bleu, which she'd briefly attended before settling down to real life. She always found herself watching him whenever he was on-screen, even when someone else was the focus of the scene. She'd never met a man like that. Or, rather, if she had, he hadn't even noticed her. Men like Kai went for women like Felicity.

Felicity grabbed a pen and paper from a nearby table and began to scribble down the URL splashed on the screen.

"What are you doing?" Addison asked.

"Sending you on an adventure."

Addison stared at her, horror dawning. Felicity was going to make her apply—so she could be humiliated and rejected. Kai was her fantasy man. *Base Camp* was her favorite escape from her mundane life. And Felicity was going to ruin it. "No," she sharply. "No, no, no, no, no."

"Oh, yes," Felicity countered, her grin growing wider. "I think it's high time we really shook up your life."

CHAPTER TWO

"I GOT THE strangest call yesterday," Renata announced, making Kai jump when she slipped into the kitchen behind him. How she'd managed to sneak up on him was anyone's guess; her ridiculous high heels tippity-tapped everywhere she went. For a second he thought someone had tipped her off to the state of their food supply, but he quickly realized that wasn't likely. As far as he knew, Angus had only told Boone so far. Kai was supposed to sneak away and meet up with them later to brainstorm ideas for how to guard the gardens and greenhouses. Then they'd tell the others.

"Oh yeah?" He turned back to the ingredients he'd laid out for a breakfast quiche.

"Yeah. Guess who it was?"

"I don't know, Renata." If he didn't keep working, breakfast wouldn't be served on time. She'd already thrown off his flow. In his head he'd been narrating the cooking process, as if he were already on a televised cooking show, talking about using local vegetables in season—

"David Linkley."

Kai stopped. Turned around. "Why'd he call you?"

"Because we go way back, and when one of the stars of my show tries to make a deal with another network while still working for me, he figured I'd want to know about it."

Hell. Not good, Kai thought as he searched for a way to answer Renata without incensing her any more. She was right; he'd approached Linkley recently, hoping to interest the man in his cooking show project.

"I'm just planning for the future. *Base Camp* will be done long before I start anything new." He hadn't done anything wrong putting out some feelers. Anyone working a television job had to be thinking about what came next.

David Linkley had reached out to Renata. That was interesting.

The man was a kingmaker among cooking shows. Had he liked Kai's hook?

Or hated it?

"You don't know that," Renata pointed out. "Maybe there'll be a sequel. *Base Camp 2—Sustainable Babies*."

A sequel?

He'd never thought of that—and he'd bet no one else had, either. All the men and women at Base Camp were planning for their futures. Since none of them had wanted to be on a reality television show in the first place, he doubted any of them would miss it when it was over.

"A sequel won't work. It won't hold an audience—

there wouldn't be a bad guy to make things interesting." During this "season" of the show, Base Camp's very existence was in question. Fulsom wouldn't be able to pull that off twice. "I'm sorry if I stepped on your toes, Renata," he went on. "I'm new to the whole television thing, but I'm aiming for a future in it. I think I've got something to tell the world."

"Why the hell didn't you bring your idea to me?" she demanded.

"You're busy. And you do reality TV. I need someone who focuses on cooking shows." It would take an expert in the field to help raise him above all the other contenders.

"You're looking to be a hit." She nodded. "I can see that. You just might make it, the way you're pursuing it."

Her compliment caught him off guard. Usually Renata was looking for a way to stick the knife in your jugular.

"Okay, here's what we'll do," she went on. "I'll tell David he can work with you to film a pilot episode—on two conditions. One, you don't even think about going into production on a series before this show ends."

"Of course." Kai's pulse kicked up. Renata was going to help him? That could be the break he needed—

"And two, we document every step of the process as you try to get your show."

"NO. I'M NOT wearing a bikini. And I'm not getting a spray tan," Addison said, her voice skidding up the scale to almost a shriek. She had a thing about bikinis. Her body didn't fit in them right. Not like Felicity's. Kai was going to look at this video. Even if she never found out what he thought about it, this was torture, because she could imagine a million reactions he might have to seeing her bathing-suit-clad body.

None of them good.

"Wait—was that a *no* I heard? Evan—get that listing up!" Felicity called.

"Evan isn't even here," Addison pointed out. They were still alone in Felicity's enormous penthouse; Evan was out of town for the weekend. Addison had woken up cranky. This yes thing was getting out of hand.

Last night she'd tossed and turned thinking about Felicity's latest campaign to drive her crazy. She could barely admit how much it hurt to have her secret attachment to *Base Camp* and Kai tampered with like this. She should tell her sister, but that meant admitting that she preferred a fantasy world to her reality. Felicity would jump all over that and tell her it was exactly why she needed to change her situation.

"Do you want the penthouse or not?"

"Yes. Yes, I want the damn penthouse. Fine, I'll wear a bikini and humiliate myself. This is never going to work, you know." She eyed the tiny swimsuit Felicity passed to her. Could it possibly contain her breasts, or would they spring free at the first jiggle and take out someone's eye?

"It's definitely going to work. Now, come on; we've got to get to the studio."

Felicity grabbed her purse and keys, leaving Addison to trail behind her, asking, "What studio? Felicity? What studio?"

"Cam's—my friend. The one I told you about."

"The independent film producer? The one who won that award?" She struggled to keep up as Felicity strode toward the elevator.

"That's right. He's totally broke, so he's going to produce this film for peanuts. Just go with the flow, okay? Act natural. You'll be fine."

"I can't believe you're getting him to help make this film," Addison said. "I'm supposed to submit a little video—something I record on my phone. Isn't this overkill?" *Please let Felicity agree*, she begged whatever deity was listening. It was one thing if Kai turned down a grainy homemade video she shot.

Another thing altogether to have a professional video tossed away.

What if they showed Kai's reactions to her video on the show? What if she had to watch him watch her—?

"Sometimes overkill is what it takes," Felicity said.

Addison was still in shock an hour and a half later as she stood in front of a green screen, dressed in a string bikini, holding a surf board and a pair of knitting needles.

"I love the sea, and I love knitting, too," she read off the teleprompter Cam had placed several feet in front of her. "I combine my two hobbies by creating ocean-themed knit caps for surfers. Everyone knows you lose most of your heat through your head, so when you've been catching too many waves, and hypo-thermia's setting in, reach for a—" she swallowed hard "—for an Addison Surf Cap and warm your vibe!"

Five bulked-up men in wetsuits peeled down to their waists to expose their muscular, wet chests and walked in front of the camera, each of them sporting a colorful knitted cap.

Addison choked. "Are you kidding me, Felicity? I can't say, *warm your vibe*. And where'd these guys come from? Where'd you get the hats?"

"Cut! Cut!" Cam called. "This is amateur hour," he accused Felicity. "You said one take and we'd be done."

"Darling, relax. This is art we're making," Felicity soothed him and turned to Addison. "Sweetie, we're trying to woo Kai Green—surf god. I did some re-search. Apparently, he likes his women to be creative, free thinkers. He wants them to care about others. We're killing two birds with one stone."

"This is—"

"A *yes*," Felicity reminded her. "From the top. Re-member, you're not Addison Reynolds; you're Addison Jones. I've got a friend working on your website and social media accounts. Kai will never know who you really are."

With a groan, Addison took her place again and shrieked when Cam chucked a bucketful of water at her. "It'll have more verisimilitude," he told Felicity as Addison gasped and flicked water from her fingertips.

More something, Addison thought. It was cold in here. She was soaked. She crossed her arms protectively over her chest and managed to jab her ear with a knitting needle.

Her fantasy man was going to see her nipples.

She was never going to watch *Base Camp* again.

"I'VE GOT THREE women for you to choose from," Boone announced to Kai several days later. He leaned in the kitchen doorway, and Kai began to think he needed another job—one that hid him far out on the ranch where no one could easily find him. Boone wasn't letting up about this bride thing, and Renata had a cameraman focused on him twenty-four seven. He had a feeling it was only going to get worse. It didn't help he was short of sleep. He'd been one of the men patrolling last night after the film crew went home. He'd steal a catnap this afternoon, but he was far from sharp right now.

"Only three?" That was a blow to his ego. Kai went back to work churning milk into butter. He had a new respect for his forebears. This chore took way too much time every day.

"I narrowed them down for you. Time's a ticking." Boone tapped his watch. "You've already lost five of your forty days."

"Narrowed them down?" He didn't like the idea of Boone sorting through women for him. What did Boone know about his preferences—his real preferences, not the baloney he'd spouted when Boone had asked him to come up with characteristics for his future wife?

"Yep. See if you like any of them." Boone set the laptop he was carrying on the kitchen counter, opened it up and showed him three links. "Each one has a video. If none of them suit, I'll send you more. I just have a good feeling about these ladies."

"Later, okay? I'm pretty busy here." He indicated the churn. He couldn't say what made him want to put this off. Maybe because every time he dated it was disaster—and it didn't help that a cameraman was practically breathing down his neck, focusing on the laptop on the counter.

"Take your time, and let me know what you think when you get a chance to watch them. But watch them soon, okay?"

Kai managed to ignore the laptop for ten minutes after Boone left, frustrating the cameraman behind him, if his sighs and fidgeting sounds were anything to go on. Kai needed to finish the butter then get busy prepping a stir-fry for lunch. He felt it his duty to feed healthy meals to the men and women in his charge. He'd noticed Savannah was looking a little pale these days. She was about five and a half months pregnant, so he'd add lots of beet greens and chard to the mix. That would help her iron levels.

He glanced over at the laptop, still lifting the plunger of the churn up and down. He supposed watching the videos wouldn't take long. He imagined a few seconds of each of them would tell him if there was any spark or not.

He reached out, preparing to click on the first video.

The cameraman behind him moved closer.

Kai snatched his hand back. Knowing an audience would watch him watch these videos was creepy.

He'd look later, he decided. After the butter was done. After lunch. When he was alone.

If he was ever alone again.

Kai went back to churning.

He glanced over his shoulder a few minutes later. The cameraman was still hovering. He couldn't help glance at the laptop again, too. What kind of women answered wife-wanted ads anyway? Desperate ones?

Weird ones?

Serial killers?

Kai lifted the plunger up and down, but his gaze kept straying to where the laptop perched on the counter. Finally, he slammed his plunger down. Better just watch the damn things before he overthought it. Audience or no audience.

He moved the laptop closer, tapped the keyboard to bring it back to life and clicked the top link. The cameraman inched even closer.

A woman in business attire with short cropped curly hair and a pleasant smile, standing in front of a full bookcase, said, "Hi, I'm Linda, and I'm a successful author of self-help books. I teach my clients and readers all about productivity. How to increase their output and the output of their employees, as well—"

Kai killed the video and clicked the next one, even as he acknowledged Linda was everything he'd said he wanted: creative, productive, sensible.

Sane.

But he felt absolutely no spark. And he couldn't marry without that. Couldn't spend a lifetime with a woman he had no passion for.

This time a woman appeared in jeans, work boots, a flannel shirt and a hard hat. She was cute in a healthy, strong, outdoorsy way.

"Hi, I'm Candice, and I work in the construction field. I'm a whiz with most tools and would love to join Base Camp and learn all about sustainable building—"

Hell, even better. A woman with skills that could be useful here at Base Camp. She was strong, sensible, creative and sane, too—

But Kai still didn't feel even the inkling of a spark. Both the women in the videos were so... independent. What did they need a husband for?

Probably a messed-up way of thinking about marriage, Kai told himself. Men and women were supposed to be equals. Where did need come in? And why did he even want a woman who needed him?

Kai stood hunched over the laptop for a second, not wanting to follow that train of thought. Did he think a woman who needed him would be less likely to leave?

Hell.

A pressure in his chest pushed against his heart. Was he flawed in a way that couldn't be fixed?

Was he going to ruin Base Camp for everyone?

Focus on the now, he told himself. Watch the video. No sense borrowing trouble.

He reluctantly clicked the last link, then bent closer

to the screen as a woman appeared in a close-up shot. Her hair was a shimmering silver fading to dark brown. Her gray eyes stared out from an elfin face. This woman didn't match his description at all. Why had Boone included her?

Had Boone seen right through him?

As the video panned out, Kai saw she wore a string bikini—a wet string bikini that left little to the imagination, he noted, his body immediately thrumming with interest—and had one arm looped around a vintage surf board his friends back in Long Beach would kill to try out. In her other hand she held a pair of knitting needles.

There was something about her that hooked him immediately. A glance she sent at someone off-camera, a mixture of humor, desperation and exasperated disbelief he found endearing. Whoever it was must have sent a message back to get going with her video, because she turned to face the lens head on and affected a bright, cheerful pose.

"Hi, I'm Addison. I love the sea, and I love knitting, too. I combine my two hobbies by creating ocean-themed knit caps for surfers. Everyone knows you lose most of your heat through your head, so when you've been catching too many waves, and hypothermia's setting in, reach for an Addison Surf Cap and warm your vibe!"

Kai's mouth tugged up at the corner, even as his gaze dipped to her breasts again.

Addison was sexy, funny, off-beat, loony as a locoweed.

And Kai wanted her—

Bad.

"I'M AT WORK. I'm not saying yes to anything," Addison hissed into her phone. She'd been ignoring its buzz all morning, knowing it was Felicity. She'd taken a lot of crap about her hair when she came into work on Monday, although several of the women admitted they loved it when they met up with her in the break room. Management did not love it and had suggested, although not in so many words, she might want to dye it back to its normal shade.

Addison couldn't do that because Felicity made her check in each night on a video chat to make sure she hadn't. This whole thing was getting way out of hand. Currently her hair was tucked into a tight bun, and she sported a wide headband that covered most of the ombre parts. She wasn't sure if she'd made things better or worse.

The week had dragged by so slowly she could have been working on a chain gang under a desert sun. Every day she agonized over the video they'd sent in. Would Kai see it? What would he think? Would they put it on the show so everyone else she knew could ridicule her?

"You won't believe what I'm looking at," Felicity said.

"A mocha latte?" She would kill for a mocha latte. A mocha latte spiked with vodka. Or something even stronger. Something that would knock her out long enough by the time she woke up this nightmare would be over.

"A marriage proposal."

"You already have a husband." Addison pulled out the Delaney file, wishing she could offload it on a newer hire, but her boss had—

"Wait. What did you just say?" Addison's heart stopped.

"A marriage proposal. Well, okay—not quite. But it's an invitation to come on *Base Camp*. From Kai Green. You did it! You're going to be on the show! He thinks he wants to marry you!"

Addison sat back, letting the file slip from her fingers. "Felicity—" What had they done? She'd thought being turned down would be the worst thing that could happen to her.

But being asked onto the show? So that Kai could reject her in real time? "I don't want to be on TV," she cried. "Kai doesn't want me; he's looking for a *wife*."

"A fake wife," Felicity corrected her. "Don't get your panties in a twist. Reality TV shows are totally fake. No one really expects you to actually marry him."

Addison couldn't keep up. This was even worse. A moment before she'd been worried Kai would reject her. Now she was worried it wouldn't be real if they did tie the knot.

But of course it wouldn't be real. Kai Green wasn't going to marry her—no matter what.

"But they have weddings all the time on the show," she protested weakly. She had to make her sister see she couldn't go near Base Camp. She was supposed to win a year in Felicity's penthouse. That was the goal. Marrying Kai was—

A fantasy. Pure and simple. It would never happen, real or fake. And going on *Base Camp* had nothing to do with her real life—or her dreams. It took place on a ranch, for God's sake. Where there were bison. And people slept in tents.

She was angling for a city life—one brimming with excitement. She wanted to throw events for the stars. Never mind she had no idea how to get from here to there. She was positive moving to New York was the first step. Moving to Montana and letting Kai blow her self-esteem to smithereens?

Not on the menu.

"Fake weddings," Felicity insisted. "I know what I'm talking about; I'm the one with friends in the industry, right? Nothing you see on those episodes is real."

"But—" Addison wasn't sure Felicity was right. The couples on the show lived together, slept together, got up in the morning together. She didn't think it was fake. Heck, Savannah and Jericho were having a baby.

"Besides, your month is up in twenty-four days. You can bail on the show well before the wedding. Think of it; by the time you get to Base Camp you'll have less than three weeks left. Less than three weeks to flirt and play with Kai Green! Then, poof! You disappear, they scramble around to find another fake bride and it'll be great television. You'll be doing them a favor!"

"What about me?" She didn't think Kai would consider being dumped a favor. She remembered how Curtis had acted when Harris had stolen his bride. He'd been crushed.

Or had that been an act, too?

"What about you? You're saying yes to life, remember? You'll be able to put 'actress' on your résumé. People in New York will love that. Come on, Addison, you haven't done anything exciting in years. Not since you came home from the Cordon Bleu. This is your chance. Quit your job. Throw all your cares to the wind. Give up your lease. Sell your stuff. Store the rest of it at my place. I'm making a big change; isn't it time you made one, too?"

"But—"

"Come on. Say the word. I'll arrange everything. Remember my penthouse.... It's waiting for you. Will you do it?"

It was like standing at the edge of a precipice, Addison thought, and the one person in the world who was supposed to love you wasn't handing you a lifeline.

She was pushing you off the cliff.

But Kai Green was waiting at the bottom of it—whether to catch her or watch her fall, she didn't know.

That was the risk. Was she willing to take it?

Addison took a deep breath.

"Yes."

CHAPTER THREE

"KAI, YOU KNOW all we've ever wanted was for you to be happy," Wanda said.

"I know. I'm trying. Like I told you, I'm working on getting a cooking show." Kai was perfectly sure his adoptive mother wanted things to work out for him, but sometimes he wondered if happiness was hereditary. Everyone in the Ledbetter family seemed to be born knowing what they wanted and how to go about getting it. Wanda and Eric were medical researchers. His brother, Gary, worked for the Red Cross. Celia was married now with three children who took up almost all her time. She was going to night school to finish her teaching degree, however.

Grace, his biological sister, was happy, too, he reminded himself. She had been working for Child Protective Services since she graduated from college. A job she'd chosen because she was determined to protect children in circumstances like the one she and Kai had once been in. Now she had Tom to share her life with. Maybe genes had nothing to do with it.

"Being a television star is an interesting aspiration, but is it really all you want to do?"

He knew what she meant. The Ledbetter motto was *Service*, with a capital S.

"I'm cooking for a bunch of SEALs right now," he pointed out. "Who are building a sustainable community."

"But think of the thousands of people you could help feed if you joined Gary in the Red Cross."

Kai sighed. Somehow Wanda couldn't understand his vision, and he remembered the days when he'd first signed up with the Navy. One of his more zealous friends had organized a protest on his lawn, and even his family had joined in. His parents were proponents of non-violent communication, a system they believed could solve every problem even when opponents took up arms. In Kai's eyes, they were naive. But then, he'd been naive, too. He'd gone into the service thinking he'd be able to right every wrong he came across. That hadn't been the case. Now he was trying something new.

"I want to teach thousands of people to be able to feed themselves, Mom," he said. He wished she could get on board with his plans for his future. When a Ledbetter supported you, it was like money in the bank.

"But there will always be people who can't feed themselves."

"I'm glad Gary's helping with that." His passion was different, though. And just as valid.

"I watched this week's episode of *Base Camp*," Wanda said.

Kai bit back a groan. "Mom—"

"It's your turn to get married, and you don't have a woman in sight. A wife-wanted ad isn't going to end well. You know that, right?"

"It's—"

"There has to be some way out of this mess you've gotten yourself into. I'm sure if we get someone to look at your contract…"

This was worse than he thought. Ledbetters didn't break contracts. If Wanda was suggesting it, she must think he'd really gone off course. "I don't want to get out of it," he told her, which was true. Things were going according to plan for the most part. He'd known all along his turn to marry would come, and if he was having doubts, too, that was his problem, not his mother's. Besides, Boone had already found him a bride.

Kai had been thinking about Addison all afternoon. That exasperated look she'd sent someone off-screen. Her curvy body in that wet bikini. Knitted surf caps. Who thought of things like that? He loved her hair— she was obviously artistic. In fact, he liked the whole package. It had been several months since he'd had anything like a girlfriend, and his body was letting him know he missed being close to a woman.

He'd like to get close to Addison.

"But marrying a stranger? Someone you find in an ad? That doesn't make any sense. What I'd suggest—"

Kai knew he had to stop Wanda before she said too

much. He was in this for good. He wasn't going to let his friends down. Nor was he going to lose this opportunity to get his lucky break. There were far worse women he could marry than Addison Jones. He'd poured over her website and social media accounts. She was quirky, interesting, down to earth, with a loopy sense of humor. She believed in fate.

So did he.

His gut told him Addison could be the one.

"Take what you're given and make something great out of it, Mom. Remember?"

"Sometimes fate needs a helping hand. Sometimes it's taught you a lesson several times over and is going to keep teaching it until you learn some sense!"

Her words conjured up the doubts he'd just managed to squash, and Kai's temper flared. Didn't she realize how much he wanted this?

Kai stilled. He himself hadn't realized how much he wanted this until just now. He'd known he'd need a wife since he joined Base Camp, and some part of him had felt agreeable to that, but this was the first time he'd understood it went further than that.

He wanted a partner—for life.

Kai made himself sit with that, even as his mother continued to talk on the other end of the line. He wanted someone permanent.

And Addison had stepped forward.

Now everything within him yearned to give a relationship with her a try. He would meet her halfway. Give it his all.

"Mom, listen. It's too late to break my contract. I'm all in on this." He braced himself, knowing the storm was about to hit.

But, as usual, Wanda kept her cool. He could almost imagine her taking deep, calming breaths. "Kai, you've proven time and time again you'll go your own way, so I'm going to give you one piece of advice and then I'll keep my own counsel."

"What's that?" he asked weakly.

"Just don't pick your usual type."

Too late, Kai thought as he said his goodbyes and hung up.

Besides, Angus had asked for drama.

Kai had a feeling he was going to get it.

"YOU CAN LEAVE in seventeen days. Remember that," Felicity said as she looked over everything Addison had packed for her trip to Montana. For once Felicity looked nervous, and Addison thought it had finally sunk in what she'd done. Dispatching your sister to marry a stranger was pretty drastic, even if you were trying to shake things up in her life.

"I know." She was almost two weeks into her month-long experiment, and so far saying yes had gone better than she'd expected. Except for the fact one of the other women at work had figured out she was being particularly agreeable these days and kept asking her to write extra reports for her.

All that was over now, though. She was back at Felicity's place getting ready to leave. The show had given her one week to report to Chance Creek, Montana, and the past seven days had gone by in a flash. Yesterday had been her last day at work. Meanwhile, she'd sold most of her possessions in whirlwind of tag sales and online ads, and packed the rest in boxes to be stored in Felicity's guest bedroom. Her suitcase held only her new, flowy, *abandoned-waif* clothes and a few extras— including some knitting needles and yarn, which Addison could now use in an elementary way thanks to the online instruction videos Felicity had forced her to watch and practice to.

"You don't want to be caught out on the first day," Felicity had pointed out.

Addison was pretty sure she'd be caught out in the first minute. She had to admit she was intrigued by the thought of meeting Kai, though. What kind of guy went for a woman who knitted surfer caps? Surely other women had applied. Women with real life skills. Who wore real clothes—had real jobs.

Or maybe not. Maybe she was the only one with a sister who wanted to ruin her life.

Remember the penthouse, she told herself. The beautiful penthouse. She was changing her life. All she had to do was make it through the next seventeen days—have a bit of an adventure. A lark. Something to tell her grandkids about. This was all fake. She'd meet Kai. Let him know she was in on the joke. They'd have a few laughs, take long walks around the ranch. Look at the bison. Swim in the creek. Pretend to flirt on camera.

And if he hated her, she'd pretend none of it fazed

her one bit. Then come home and hide in Felicity's penthouse until it blew over.

I'm going to live in Manhattan. I'm going to find a job as an event planner until I earn enough to open my own business.

Addison's Events.

She could see it now.

But on the way down to the lobby to await their ride to the airport, Addison's heart was in her mouth. She'd given up everything she'd known for this. And in just a few hours she'd meet the man who'd picked her to be his wife. It had occurred to her that despite her fears the show had never set up a woman to be dumped on-screen. So maybe there was hope this would go well.

Maybe Kai had taken one look at her video and fallen head over heels in love with her.

Get real, she told herself. *Kai doesn't want you. He simply needs you to play a role. He's a nice guy. You're a nice girl. Go to Base Camp and have a nice time.*

If only she thought there was any hope of that.

KAI WISHED HE'D been allowed to drive to the airport alone to pick up Addison, but of course that wasn't an option. Ever since the cooking show revelation, Renata hadn't left him alone for a minute. There'd been extra interviews about his aspirations and more film coverage of all the ways he folded sustainable practices into his cooking. At least it had kept him busy. And kept her from noticing the way he was stretching the food they had to cover the vegetable deficit. So far the film crew hadn't noticed their new patterns of patrolling at night, although he'd heard the crew commenting on the number of naps people were taking during the day.

Still, he'd had plenty of time to overthink this meeting.

As he stood in the waiting area of the Chance Creek Regional Airport—the closest he could get to the plane Addison was due in on—he couldn't help wondering if he really had what it took to make a marriage work. His track record with women was abysmal so far. Why did he think this time would be any different?

Maybe it was better he had an entourage with him; otherwise he might hop back into the truck and take off.

He glanced back and took in the crew members who'd ridden along with him to the airport. At least Curtis was here, too, for moral support. He wondered if the man was remembering the time he hadn't gone to the airport to pick up his bride—and Harris had stolen her.

Kai turned to face the bank of windows looking out over the tarmac, wondering for the millionth time what Addison would be like. What kind of a woman blithely promised to marry a man she hadn't met? Addison must have watched *Base Camp*—must have watched him.

And liked what she saw enough to want to spend the rest of her life with him.

That took courage—or a kind of thoughtlessness that boggled the mind.

He supposed he'd find out which it was soon enough.

"I see the plane," Curtis said. "Only a few minutes

now."

Those minutes stretched out endlessly, but finally the plane touched town and taxied to park near the terminal. A few moments later, the door to the plane opened and passengers began to file out and down the stairs onto the tarmac.

"There she is," Curtis said, but Kai had already seen Addison. How could you miss the lovely waif among the soccer moms, businessmen and couples with young children?

Just as before, his pulse picked up when he caught sight of her. It was a breezy day, and her dress clung to her body, revealing a figure that set fire to his imagination.

Addison said something to the stewardess at the top of the stairs, and they both laughed, the stewardess looking as charmed with Addison as Kai felt. There was that sense of humor he'd glimpsed at the start of her video. And there was that bohemian fashion sense that had caught his fancy, too.

"I hate to say this, buddy," Curtis interrupted his thoughts. "But she's not going to make it a day at Base Camp. Look at her. A strong wind would blow her away. What does a woman like that know about hard work and primitive conditions?"

Kai understood what Curtis was saying—Addison wasn't dressed for ranch life. She was wearing some sort of flowy, gauzy number that looked as substantial as a spiderweb. But he liked the way she looked. Hell, he'd gladly shoulder her workload as well as his, if it meant she'd stick around.

Addison was beautiful, her face alight with interest as she descended the stairs. Then something caught her gaze, and Kai watched as she stepped off the bottom tread and darted forward to catch a toddler who'd swayed on his feet and nearly sat down hard on the tarmac. With a smile and a laugh, she returned the child to his father, who'd let go of the toddler's hand for a moment to adjust the carryon he was juggling, along with an umbrella stroller under his other arm.

A second later, she helped a woman retrieve a silky, bright-red scarf that had slipped from her shoulder. Addison was the kind of woman who paid attention, Kai decided, more attracted to her than ever. Someone who took care of the people around her. She was slim, but athletic rather than delicate, he noticed, and he thought Curtis was underestimating her. She was still keeping an eye on the errant toddler ahead of her, and Kai could tell she was making sure the little boy reached the door safely.

Then her gaze lifted—

And caught his.

Kai's mouth went dry.

He took in the mischief lighting her eyes, her delight in the antics of the toddler swinging on his father's arm and the way her smile spread into a conspiratorial grin when she saw him. Every nerve in his body woke up, sending the alert it was time to make this woman his. Then her gaze slid to the cameramen behind him, who were filming every second of her approach. Her smile faltered, faded, and Kai's stomach sank. If she didn't like cameras, Curtis was right; she wouldn't last a day—

But the next moment a smile tugged up one corner of her mouth, and she glanced back at him. The mischief was back as she lifted a shoulder and almost rolled her eyes. That gesture encompassed the absurdity of the moment and included him in her desire to laugh at it. Kai held his breath. She wasn't fighting it; simply acknowledging it, as if to say, "Well, all we can do is put up with this circus."

Kai was hooked.

He moved forward to greet her as she came through the door, wanting to be closer to her. "Addison? I'm—"

"Kai," she said, and her smile lit up her eyes. "Of course. You look just like you do on TV." Color suffused her cheeks, and Kai's breath hitched again. She was attracted to him, and he felt an answering surge in his blood. "Now I sound like a groupie," Addison added.

"Nah," he said, wanting to set her at ease. "I'm glad you watch the show. It means you know me."

"Do you think so?"

When their gazes met, Kai was utterly sure she did. He wished he could reach out and touch her—

And then he did.

Her skin was soft under his thumb, and as he stroked it down her jaw, her eyes widened.

He dropped his hand to his waist, suddenly conscious again of the cameras filming all of this.

"You're beautiful," he managed, hoping like hell he

didn't sound like an ass. She was, though. It seemed important to tell her.

"Th—thanks." She watched him warily, as if unsure whether to believe him.

Could he kiss her?

No. Not yet.

Soon though.

He realized his gaze had dropped to her mouth and that she'd noticed. She was holding her breath.

"I guess... we'd better get your baggage." His voice was husky. He hoped she knew he would have said a lot more if they weren't being filmed. "You must be tired."

Hell, if he'd wanted to keep his head, he wasn't doing a very good job of it. He was falling for Addison. Had fallen halfway already. He might be cool under pressure and know how to harness meditation to find his way to being one with the world, but when it came to women he was binary. He was either all-in or all-out where relationships were concerned. With Addison, he was all-in.

Maybe the universe knew how to provide when it came to women, after all.

"Didn't sleep much last night," she admitted. "Not sure I'll sleep tonight, either."

Not if he had anything to do with it.

Kai caught himself. They'd just met, and this wasn't someone he'd picked up at a bar. This was a woman he'd promised to marry, even if he hadn't officially proposed yet.

"Come on."

Kai took her hand without thinking, but her touch ignited a jolt of hunger inside him. This felt right, he told himself as he led her across to the baggage carousel.

"Just ignore the crew," he said as the camera people made way for them to pass.

"That's not easy." She kept sliding glances their way and put her other hand up to smooth her hair. He knew how she felt. The first few days of filming he'd been so self-conscious he'd kept tripping over his own feet.

"It gets easier as you go."

"Do you ever forget they're there?"

"No."

He liked the way she smiled at his truthful answer. He had a feeling even Wanda would like her. But then she'd take Addison under her wing, get her set up with a life plan and start coaching her about goals and scheduling.

He'd hold off introducing them for a bit. First things first: get Addison's bag and get her home.

"This is Curtis Lloyd," he said when he realized his friend was waiting for an introduction. "You've probably seen him on the show, too."

"I have. I hope you get your turn soon, Curtis."

Curtis shrugged. He liked to pretend he was unconcerned about his future, but Kai suspected he worried about finding a wife as much as any of them. Maybe more.

"Was your trip okay?" Kai asked Addison. He needed to find solid ground. The strength of his reaction to her had knocked him off-kilter, and it was time to bring things back to normal, if possible.

"It was fine. I've never been to Montana before. It was beautiful when we were descending toward the airport. It's so sparsely populated. There aren't a lot of people here, are there?"

Both men chuckled at that. "This is definitely the country," Kai explained. "You know what you're signing up for, right?"

"Of course." But Addison didn't look so sure. Kai bit back a surge of concern. He didn't want to lose her. What if she hated Base Camp? Hated the life he'd pledged himself to? One thing at a time, he decided. Get her back to Base Camp. Get her settled. She'd do fine, he assured himself.

When they reached the truck, Addison greeted Curtis's dog, Daisy, like an old friend. Harris and Sam had found Daisy on their wedding day, but the dog loved to follow Curtis everywhere. Kai's heart warmed as he saw the way the mutt greeted the new arrival. If Daisy approved of Addison, she had to be a good person.

A half hour later, they pulled in at Base Camp to find the rest of the inhabitants waiting near the fire pit to be introduced. Kai could only guess how intimidating it was to meet everyone at once, but Addison seemed to take it in stride. As she shook hands all around, it became clear she knew them all from the TV show.

"I love your dresses," she told the women, who were wearing their traditional Regency outfits. Kai supposed Addison knew the history of that choice since she watched the show regularly.

"We'll get you measured up for some gowns of your own," Savannah told her.

"I can't wait," Addison confessed to her. "One of my favorite parts of the show is seeing what you all are wearing."

"It's so weird knowing people really watch us," Savannah said to Avery as Addison moved on.

Avery nodded. "I like her, though," Kai heard her whisper.

"Do we seem crazy on the show?" Riley asked Addison.

"No," Addison said. "You all seem really nice. I hate it when the hour is over. It's like you all are so alive, while my life is just... boring."

"Boring?" Kai echoed. "You make hats for surfers. That's awesome."

"Right." Color rose in Addison's cheeks. "But... I don't build tiny houses, or run a Regency bed-and-breakfast, or work with solar panels, or..." She waved a hand to encompass all of them.

Kai was gratified by her enthusiasm and the way the rest of Base Camp's inhabitants seemed to be warming to her. It would make all the difference in Addison's experience of the place if people accepted her. Still, this had to be a lot to take in all at once. He could see the strain on her face as other people leaned in to ask her questions.

Kai moved closer, pretending to himself he was only thinking of her when he angled to get her alone. "Want to go on a walk? Just the two of us?"

"And the cameras?" she asked, raising an eyebrow.

"Of course. Like I said, they're always there. They'll hang back, though. It's quieter out in the woods."

"Okay. That sounds good." But he noticed she was twisting her hands in the strings of her purse. Was she nervous?

Afraid to be alone with him?

Maybe he was pushing this too fast.

"A walk sounds like a great idea. We'll stop over-whelming you," Boone told Addison. "Everyone, back to work," he called out.

Groans sounded from the gathered crowd, then scattered laughter, and people began to disperse. Most of the women traipsed up to the Manor. Samantha headed toward the gardens, and Avery joined Walker on the way to the barns. Only Boone and Riley hung back.

"We'll leave your stuff in the bunkhouse and set up your tent later," Kai told Addison. He grabbed her bags from the back of the truck and led the way into the building. Addison, following, took in the large open room, which in its past would have been filled with bunk beds to house the single hired hands on the ranch. She peeked through an open door toward the kitchen. Kai realized she'd seen all this before on the show.

"We'll spend plenty of time in there later," he as-sured her.

"I've got an appointment set up for Addison with Alice Reed after lunch," Riley said. She and Boone had trailed after them into the bunkhouse. "For your clothes," she told Addison.

Addison nodded.

"We'd better hurry if we're going to get that walk before it's time to start cooking lunch," Kai said and took her hand.

"Would you like to help Kai with the meals?" Boone asked Addison. "Everyone has job assignments here, but we didn't assign you one yet. Do you like to cook? Or is there something else you're interested in?"

"I love to cook," Addison said. "I went to the Cordon Bleu for a year."

Kai brightened. "Really? That's amazing." He wondered why she hadn't mentioned it in her video.

"I didn't get to finish my training. Ran out of cash," Addison said. "Someday I'd like to go back."

"Well, you can help me as much as you like. I don't do a lot of fancy cooking, but maybe you'll have some ideas we can incorporate."

"I'd like to help out in the B and B, too, if that's okay," she added shyly. "Do you think the other women would mind?"

"Mind?" Riley said. "Heck, no. We need all the help we can get."

"That's decided then," Boone said.

Kai led the way back outside and down the track toward Pittance Creek, which ran through the property.

"You're from Connecticut, right?" he asked, remembering something he'd realized only after looking at her application several times.

"That's right."

"How'd you get into knitting hats for surfers?"

"Oh… I travel out to California whenever I can."

"What's your favorite surf—"

"What do you do in your spare time? When the cameras aren't on you?" she blurted.

Kai was taken aback but recovered quickly. "I… like to cook."

There was that impish smile again. "You do that on camera all the time," she pointed out. "I mean when you're on your own."

He supposed she was right; he couldn't really call cooking his hobby anymore. He searched for something else to tell her. Something real to share with her so she'd know he was taking this seriously. "I bird watch." There. That was something no one else here knew. Renata would have a field day when she saw this clip.

"You do?" Her smile widened into a grin again. "That's… different."

Kai relaxed a little. He realized he was bracing himself for the moment when she realized she didn't want him. "Yeah. I keep a record of what I see. I always have. I'm not obsessive; I just like to know who's around."

"Cool," she said, tilting her head to look in the treetops, as if there might be a whole congregation of birds up there right now. "What kind of birds have you seen since you've been here?"

"A heck of a lot of crows," he said ruefully.

"Of course," she said as if she knew about these things. She kept walking, her head tilted back, and Kai had a sudden, dizzying urge to kiss her. First on her mouth, then he'd trace his lips down her throat. He imagined her face flushed with desire. Her eyes shining with want—

Kai shook off the thought. Hell, he needed to get himself in hand.

"Jays, woodpeckers, a peregrine falcon—all kind of birds, really," he made himself go on. "I'll show you my list."

"I'd like that."

They walked in silence, both of them scanning the treetops and listening to the sounds of the forest—and the footsteps of the camera crew behind them. Kai squeezed her hand, and she squeezed back, sending a pulse of desire straight through him. The cameras couldn't pick that up, and it was damn lucky they couldn't read his mind. He liked feeling he and Addison had a way to communicate that was just theirs.

If only he could tell her how badly he wanted to get close to her. He was such a basket of hormones; his libido had gone crazy. All Kai could think about was getting Addison into a far more intimate situation.

Soon, he promised himself. Once they knew each other better, he'd get her alone and act on his impulses. He knew she'd be sweet to the taste. Had a feeling they'd fit together well.

Cool your jets, he told himself. He was finding a wife. And he'd just met Addison; he needed to let things spin out until he figured out who she really was. What made her tick.

It was one thing to marry to secure the ranch for Base Camp.

It was another thing to hitch his wagon to a woman who might take him on a wild ride to nowhere. He reminded himself of all his past failures. This time he had to take it slow to make it work.

Although he didn't have a lot of time.

At the creek they sat on the bank, and when he pulled his shoes off to dangle his feet in the cold water, she followed suit.

"Can I ask you a question?" Addison angled her head to look at him.

"Sure." If he was going to be her husband, he couldn't hide anything from her.

"Why me?"

ADDISON HELD HER breath as she waited for his answer. Sitting here on this creek bed, dangling her feet in the water, a crew of cameramen filming her as she talked to her supposed fiancé—all of this was surreal. Any moment she felt like the whole thing would stop and they'd send her home. She was light-headed. She'd appreciated Kai's steady hand holding hers as they'd walked because the truth was if he hadn't been gripping her, she felt as if she'd have lifted off the ground and floated away.

She'd been prepared for indifference on Kai's part when he'd met her. Even scorn.

Instead he kept looking at her like he wanted to—

She wasn't sure. Kiss her? Touch her?

Eat her up?

She'd definitely seen desire there, and something

else. Something like… hope. She didn't know what that meant, and she was finding it hard to breathe—or keep answering his questions.

She still didn't understand why there hadn't been a briefing when she arrived. She'd expected a trailer with a hairstylist and someone to tell her where to stand and what to say. There'd been no explanation that the whole thing was a setup—no script for her to read or activity for her to perform. Everyone had seemed as real as they'd acted on TV.

Addison was beginning to wonder if Felicity had this all wrong.

Thrust into the action, all she could do was keep going. She hadn't meant to put Kai on the spot.

But she needed to know what was going on.

Kai searched her face with his gaze, and she couldn't help thinking he was… well… beautiful, if you could call a man that. His face was all planes and angles, with wide-set crystal-blue eyes, his blond hair falling into his face. A strong chin. And his mouth.

That smile of his…

It made her insides flip whenever he looked her way.

"Was it my knitting?" she prompted him, mostly to distract herself from that last thought, and then wished she hadn't. What if Kai asked her to demonstrate? She'd really be up a creek. She was crafty enough she hadn't been half-bad after a tutorial or two, but she doubted she could reproduce a "surf cap."

"Your knitting is… great," Kai said with a lopsided

grin. "But that wasn't it." He picked up a stone and tossed it from hand to hand.

Her whole body buzzing from the effects of that grin, she stumbled on. "The bikini, then." She hoped she was pulling off this teasing thing.

"That was nice, but no." He glanced at her, and Addison's heart stopped. His gaze held something wicked in it. Something that said he'd like to see her in that bikini again sometime—when they were alone.

Her skin grew hot, and she couldn't help but look at his hands. How would he touch her—?

"Why, then?" She had to clear her throat and try twice to get the words out, and even when she did she didn't sound like herself.

"It was… you," he said after a moment's hesitation. "Everything about you."

This man could make her cry, she realized, horrified at how close she was to tearing up right now. If he was making these words up, he was cruel. Because they were slicing through all her defenses straight to the most tender part of her being.

Despite her attempts to harden herself against what must be flattery, she remembered something Felicity had once said when they were talking about how she and Evan had met. That it was Evan who had decided they'd be together; he'd fallen for Felicity in an instant and decided to spend his life with her right then and there.

"He saw me and knew I was the one. Then didn't take no for an answer. Not in a creepy way. Just in a way that told me how serious he was. He had this utter belief in us. It still holds us together."

Addison hadn't known what to think of that. Felicity was right; Evan wasn't creepy. He was a successful, practical, kind of wonderful man who was so good for Felicity. But how could a person know who they were supposed to be with after a single look?

It didn't seem likely.

"The video wasn't very long," she pointed out. "It's not like you could learn that much about me from it."

"No, you're right. It doesn't make sense. I just knew." Kai put down the rock again. Stroked his thumb over her palm.

The ground dipped and tilted beneath her. Oh… hell. Addison didn't know where to look or what to do. "I'm… glad," she managed. This was potent stuff. Maybe she hadn't been around men enough lately. They usually didn't affect her like this. With each stroke of his thumb over her palm, she was growing dizzier. Hungry to get even closer to him. Kai was built like a warrior, muscled all over, but it was his gaze that undid her. She wondered what he saw when he looked at her.

"Addison—I'd like to kiss you," Kai said softly. "Can I?" It was a gentle question but a purely masculine one. She found herself unable to resist.

Besides, that had been a direct question. A question caught on camera. She had no choice: Felicity would be watching the show when it aired.

Addison looked at the handsome SEAL, screwed up her courage and said, "Yes."

CHAPTER FOUR

ADDISON TASTED AS sweet as melon dipped in honey, and once he started kissing her, Kai didn't want to stop. In fact, he wanted to lay her down and explore much more of her.

But this was their first kiss, and they were being filmed. So eventually, but not too quickly, he exercised restraint and pulled back. Addison opened her eyes, gray as storm-tossed skies, and the look she gave him made his pulse throb.

She felt the same way. He was sure of it.

Which made him want her all the more.

One of the camera crew inched nearer, and Kai got a hold of himself. "Lunch," he said huskily. "We'd better go back." It was torture to stand up and break the spell of the moment. Instead he wanted to kiss Addison again. To explore her reaction to him.

But not now. Not with an audience.

"Isn't it early?" Addison asked, following him.

"Time to make it," he explained, looking back over his shoulder.

"Oh, right. Of course." She sounded breathless, like their encounter had knocked her off-guard, too. He couldn't help but reach out and twine his fingers around hers. She let him, which told him he had to be at least partly right.

But the not-knowing was already getting to him. Maybe Addison would be like every other woman he'd dated. Maybe she'd grow restless and leave—

He remembered a lecture his father had given him back when he was still in high school and he'd come home devastated that a pretty girl named Isobel had dumped him mid-party for another boy.

"Everyone wants the gorgeous girls, the fragile ones, the femme fatales," Eric Ledbetter had said. "But most of the time, they aren't worth the drama. Look for the sensible ones. Give them a chance. Most of them are pretty, too, and what's more, they're fun to be with. They won't lead you around like a pet goat. They'll partner with you, join in with you, play sports with you—do stuff. I wish you could hear me, Kai. It would save you a world of hurt."

Kai sighed. Addison was anything but sensible. She was as quirky as all the other women he'd dated in his life. He wasn't sure why he'd reacted like he had; she wasn't going to stay—

Kai stumbled. Stopped in his tracks. Turned Addison to face him.

"Are you going to stay?"

He immediately wished he could take back his words. He'd never exposed himself like this while being filmed. The camera crew, who'd fallen back, rushed to take up positions around them, sensing a story.

Addison opened her mouth to speak, faltered, bit her lip and hesitated so long he thought she'd never answer. When she spoke, it was in a tone he couldn't quite interpret.

"Yes."

She pulled away from him and resumed walking, picking up speed as she went.

Kai followed her, half relieved, half filled with anxiety. She hadn't sounded sure, no matter what she'd said. Now she was practically running from him.

But wasn't that to be expected? She'd just got here.

He needed to back off. Give her room to get used to Base Camp—and him.

Instead, he strode after her, soon caught up with her and twined his fingers with hers again, needing to prove to himself he was master of this situation. She didn't pull away, and he hoped that meant something.

When they reached the bunkhouse kitchen, Addison slipped from his grip and moved quickly to wash her hands. "Do you have an extra apron?" she asked with a glance at the camera crew, who'd followed them.

"Over there." He pointed to a hook on the wall. "Want to dice some onions for me?"

"Sure."

Once she'd tied on an apron, she fetched the onions, a knife and a cutting board, moving around the kitchen as if she'd lived here for years. When she noticed him watching, she said, "Relax, sailor—I can dice an onion. I swear. Cordon Bleu, remember?"

Kai chuckled. "Right. I'll leave you to it." He decided to let go of his worries for now. He couldn't force an answer out of her, and he might as well enjoy spending time with a pretty woman while he could.

He got to work on the rest of the meal, a chili that was good, hearty fare for a cool fall day. After a few minutes, he lost himself in browning the meat.

"Garlic?" Addison asked a few minutes later.

"Um-hmm."

"Green peppers?"

"That's right." When he finally turned to help Addison, he found she'd prepped all the vegetables—quite nicely, too. "You're a pro, aren't you?"

"Oh." Addison blinked. "Well, you know—knitting is my real love."

SHE NEEDED TO remember who she was—and who she was supposed to be. Cooking could be one of her hobbies, but she was Addison the surf-cap maker, the artsy kind of girl Kai liked to pursue—not the practical cook and party-thrower who could feed fifty people as easily as three. Felicity had told her to play down her cooking skills.

"Men don't want competition; they want someone who complements them. Don't tell him you're a whiz in the kitchen."

She guessed she'd already messed up.

Her short stint at cooking school had come about through savings from her high school jobs. When the cash had run dry, Addison had gone home, gone back to work and put herself through business school night courses.

It was nice to work in the kitchen with a real chef again, and she appreciated Kai's flow in the way he worked, the care in the way he prepared the food—and the way he thought about the men and women who would eat it. Once the chili was bubbling on the stove, they worked on dessert. Baked apple slices with a honey drizzle. Soon delicious smells were wafting from the oven.

The rest of the inhabitants of Base Camp were far more relaxed at lunch than they'd been when she met them earlier. She enjoyed a closer look at the women's dresses and couldn't wait to get her own. She also enjoyed the way the men and women bantered. They all seemed so comfortable with one another. They had a shared history. Addison wondered if she'd ever feel like that.

Of course she wouldn't, she told herself. She was only going to be here seventeen more days. Then she'd fly back to New York, take possession of an amazing penthouse and start working to attain her dream.

"Want a tour before your fitting?" Kai asked when the meal was over and she'd helped him clean up. She was beginning to get an inkling of the full days Kai worked, barely a chance between meals to take a break before it was time to get cooking again.

"Yes," Addison said. That was an easy one to agree to.

Kai showed her the chicken house with its fenced in run and told her they got about two dozen eggs a day. Next came the horses. "Would you like to ride sometime?"

"Yes." She'd never tried riding, but she'd give it a go. She hoped Kai was a patient teacher, though.

There were pigs in a sty and bison out in the pastures. Kai said they came closer sometimes, but Addison was fine with admiring them from a distance. He took her hand as they walked to the garden.

Addison liked it when he did that. Probably too much. She'd liked it when he'd kissed her, too, more than she wanted to admit—her legs were still weak from the experience. She couldn't help hoping he'd try that again soon. He was bigger than the men she'd dated before, buff in a way that was new to her. Powerful. But gentle.

So hot she melted every time he was near.

Addison didn't think she'd ever had a crush like this in real life. She kept telling herself she'd built up Kai in her mind to be something no real man could ever be.

But this felt real.

She turned away so he couldn't see the smile she knew was tugging at her mouth. Felicity would crow if she could see her now. Addison could almost hear her. "See? Just say yes and see how much fun you can have!"

She *was* enjoying herself.

Far too much.

Would she make love to Kai before all was said and done?

She slid a look at him. Found him looking back. Heat suffused her body.

God, she hoped so.

Then she wanted to cover her face with her hands. Could he read her mind? She was in trouble if he could.

"We grow a lot of stuff," Kai went on, and Addison breathed easier, realizing she hadn't given herself away. "Boone, Samantha and Angus do most of the work. I help when I can. I love these heirloom tomatoes. Want to try one?" He bent down to pick a ripe one.

"Uh... yes?" Damn, she hated tomatoes. Addison knew that was weird; everyone else loved them, especially these old-fashioned varieties, but she'd never been able to stand them. She disliked marinara sauce, too. Try explaining that to most people. She'd choked down the chili at lunch and knew it was good, but she'd eaten it because she had to—not because she'd wanted to.

But the rules were the rules. She couldn't tell herself Felicity wouldn't find out, because the cameramen who'd trailed them all day were still following them. Reluctantly, she took the beautiful tomato, bit in and cringed.

"What's wrong?" Kai asked. "Isn't it ripe?"

Addison chewed and swallowed as fast as she could, then handed it back, wiping her mouth with the back of her hand. Ugh. God, the most tomatoey tomato she'd ever had.

Kai took a bite. "It's perfect," he said when he had swallowed. He peered at her. "You didn't like it, did you?"

"I hate tomatoes," she confessed.

"Then why did you say yes?"

All Addison could do was shrug.

"DON'T WORRY; WE'LL have her back before dinner," Riley called as she, Avery and Addison rode off in a horse-drawn carriage driven by their neighbor, James Russell. Maud, James's wife, sat in the carriage with the other women, grilling Addison until Kai worried that she'd be overwhelmed. He knew that both Maud and James were friendly—sometimes too friendly. The older couple were Regency enthusiasts, too, and had seized on the women of Base Camp as a kind of pet project the moment they'd met them. They loved to drive the women around in their carriage, run errands for them and help throw lavish Regency entertainment at the Manor. He hoped Addison knew she didn't have to tell them everything just because they asked.

"Well? What do you think?" Curtis asked as soon as the carriage rounded a bend in the road and disappeared from view. Daisy nosed around in the dirt nearby, checking now and then to make sure her master hadn't strayed too far.

"So far, so good." He didn't want to admit how good. He was afraid to jinx it.

"Maybe I should give Boone another chance to find me a wife," Curtis mused.

"Your turn will come."

"My advice to you is don't let her out of your sight until you get her to the altar. You never know who might be lurking about waiting for his chance to snatch her away." Curtis bent down and stroked Daisy's ears absently when the dog came close.

"I'll do that." He knew Curtis was joking but knew, too, that joke had its limits. Like he'd thought, Curtis still bore the scars from losing Samantha.

He didn't want to lose Addison, that was for sure, but she'd be surrounded by women at the Reed place. She'd be back in an hour or two, and he'd make sure to spend the rest of the day with her.

"Fulsom's coming for dinner," Boone told him a few minutes later when Kai entered the bunkhouse again. "Thought you'd want to know. He'll have some people with him."

Hell. "How many people? Do they expect us to feed them?" Martin Fulsom only appeared at Base Camp when he wanted publicity—and wanted to stir things up. He knew the value of controversy and drama on the show, and sometimes he liked to poke the hornets' nest and make them all a little crazy.

Kai hoped that wasn't his intention this time.

Boone shrugged. "I'm not sure. Do the best you can, I guess."

"I wonder why he's coming." He thought about their depleted food stores. They had plenty for now, of course, but unexpected guests meant produce he should be saving for the winter would disappear.

"Renata said he wants to give us some kind of pep talk."

"Why do I doubt I'll feel peppy after it?"

Curtis laughed. "Because you've ridden this merry-go-round a time or two before." He headed off to work, and Kai made his way back into the kitchen to start prepping dinner.

A moment later, Angus popped into the room and shut the door behind him again. "What's going on? I heard Fulsom's coming."

"Then you know as much as I do," Kai told him. "More mouths to feed," he added.

"I've got some potatoes started in the greenhouse. Samantha's helping."

"That will be great—in February or March when they're ready," Kai said.

"At least we've got the bison. We could probably live on one all winter."

"I think people will notice if all we eat is meat. It would hardly be sustainable if everyone did that." Base Camp was all about balance.

"Hard times call for drastic measures."

"Hopefully not that drastic yet."

"BURGUNDY IS YOUR color," Alice Reed said decidedly. "Would you like a burgundy gown?"

"Yes," Addison said happily. Burgundy had always suited her. She loved the seamstress's airy, light-filled studio in the carriage house at Two Willows, a beautiful old ranch with extensive gardens and a fascinating hedge maze.

"Or maybe forest green." Alice fingered a length of fabric. "Maybe you'd like a green one?"

No, Addison thought. She wanted burgundy. "Yes," she said with a glance at the cameras. Damn her sister.

"Or how about this?" Alice picked up another bolt of cloth, a kind of seashell gray. "This might be something to think about. Would you like a gray gown?"

"Yes." Addison wanted to scream. She didn't like the gray material at all. It would make her look sallow. The burgundy was obviously her best choice. And call her stupid; she wanted to look her best for Kai.

Alice cocked her head, studied Addison for a moment, then reached for a bolt of hot-pink fabric with yellow hearts embroidered on it. "How about this? I think it would look stunning on you!"

"Alice! That's awful." Avery hustled over from where she'd been standing with Riley near a rack of costumes.

Alice ignored her and waited for Addison's answer, rustling the cloth at Addison as if to tempt her.

There was no way she wanted a gown made of that stuff, Addison thought.

"Yes," she whispered.

"You do not want a hot-pink gown," Avery exclaimed. "Why would you say you did?"

"I... don't want to impose," Addison improvised quickly. She couldn't explain what was really going on. That was against the rules. "Whatever you think is best," she told Alice. "I'm just so happy to be here. I've watched every episode of *Base Camp*. I love looking at the gowns you sew."

Alice dropped the hot-pink fabric, mollified and

maybe a little embarrassed, although Addison wasn't sure she'd really fooled her.

"Burgundy it is for the first one, then. Don't worry; I'll make it beautiful for you."

"Thank you." Addison was relieved. This darn yes thing was going to get her in real trouble before it was all over. She allowed Alice to take her measurements and perused the costumes with the other women while Alice altered some basic underthings for her and a simple light-blue gown she already had on hand that Addison could use for the time being.

"I'll deliver several more in a few days. They'll fit you perfectly, but these will do for now," Alice told her when she was done. She helped Addison into an outfit, explaining the complicated underthings and letting her in on the secrets of Regency dress. "You'll need help getting in and out of these clothes."

"We all help each other," Avery chimed in. "After a while you get used to it."

"Thank you." Addison loved her new outfit far better than the boho clothes Felicity had picked out. Now she looked like she belonged at Westfield. She turned in a circle, getting a better view in the mirror. "I love this dress."

Riley, who was looking out the window, said, "It looks like a storm's coming. It really feels like fall, doesn't it?"

"I'll be delivering coats for all of you soon," Alice told her. "You're going to need something warmer than the light ones I made for you earlier in the year."

"That sounds wonderful," Avery told her.

"We'd better be getting back," Riley said.

Avery joined her near the door, but Alice held Addison back, scrutinizing her as if she was trying to read her intentions in her eyes.

She nodded suddenly, as if she'd found the answer she was looking for. "Do you like dancing, Addison?"

"Yes," Addison answered truthfully.

"I think it's high time Westfield threw a ball, don't you?"

"Uh... yes?" Addison didn't know if it was or not, but it sure sounded fun. She'd need to learn those fancy Regency dances, though. She loved it when the inhabitants of Base Camp performed them on the show.

"I think it should be a Halloween ball. With costumes. Don't you think?" Alice pressed her.

Addison's excitement deflated. Halloween ball? She would be gone by then. "Yes."

"Good, it's settled. You'll take care of it, won't you?" Alice was watching her with that knowing look on her face again. This was a setup, Addison realized. Alice had somehow figured her out.

But no; how could she have? She was being paranoid.

"Well?" Alice prompted. "Wouldn't you like to organize a ball?"

Organize a ball?

Addison swallowed hard. She'd give her left arm to organize a ball. For the first time she considered the fact that the women of Base Camp ran a Regency B and B—

with a ballroom.

Her fingers itched to start decorating it.

"Yes," she agreed breathlessly.

You won't be here at Halloween, a little voice in her mind pointed out.

She refused to hear it. This was a once in a lifetime opportunity. Besides, there was only one answer she could give for the next seventeen days.

CHAPTER FIVE

MOST OF THE time, Kai had the kitchen to himself almost from dawn to dusk, except when people came in and out to grab a cup of coffee or a quick snack—especially Curtis, who was often hungry and liked to hide snacks in the fridge. Now it seemed the place had become the hub of Base Camp.

It wasn't set up for so many people. A plain, rectangular room lined with cabinets and appliances, it was cramped enough at the best of times. With a full camera crew and Renata, it was tight, with all of them doing a shuffling dance out of the way any time he needed something from the refrigerator. Curtis, done with his chores for the day, had popped in mid-afternoon and hung out for a while, finally grabbing a snack to tide him over until dinner and heading off to take Daisy on a walk. The man seemed in need of company these days, and normally Kai didn't mind; but it had made dinnertime preparations a little awkward in the cramped space. Plus, an alarming amount of food disappeared every time Curtis walked out the door.

When Addison arrived in her new Regency gown, he had to put down his chopping knife and come see the full effect. She twirled around, and the smile on her face warmed his heart. She was blending into the community far more swiftly than he would have expected. In fact, when he thought about his former girlfriends placed in a similar situation, he shuddered. Kelsie would have gotten in everyone's way with her aimless wanderings. Rachel would have given him—and everyone else—a lecture on why her stand against gender roles prevented her from helping him cook. Holly and India wouldn't be caught dead in Montana, no matter what the cause.

Addison was different. Open to new experiences. Embracing them wholeheartedly. She always seemed to say yes to things.

"You don't mind having to wear that whole getup?" he asked, although she clearly didn't.

"Mind? I love it. It's so… girly. I never get to be girly."

That seemed like an odd thing to say. "The outfit you arrived in was girly. So was that bikini on your video," he pointed out. He'd looked at her video a lot when he was alone. Maybe it was chauvinistic to enjoy the way she filled out that swimsuit, but she'd sent it to him, and the bikini's wet fabric had revealed a lot.

Her cheeks pinked. "Well, sure, but you know what I mean. Not like this."

"I guess." He chalked up his inability to see the distinction to the gender divide.

"Look at my bonnet," she said and put it on, turning her head this way and that. "I've never worn a bonnet before."

"Nice." He really didn't know what else to say. He wasn't so enamored of the bonnets. They seemed silly, mostly, although he supposed in this era of skin cancer, protecting your face the sun's rays was practical.

"Nice? Argh—men," she said and turned to Curtis, who'd come back, Daisy threading through everyone's legs. "What do *you* think?"

"Absolutely stunning," Curtis pronounced with a flourish, and even the cameramen chuckled when Addison clapped.

"See? That's how you do it," she told Kai. "I guess you're more of a surfer type, though. You probably don't like the Regency thing."

She was still joking, but Kai wasn't stupid. He might be a guy, but he had enough of a radar to catch that Addison really wanted to know his feelings about the way she was dressed. He looked at her again. Really looked at her. She was right; he'd always written off the women's Regency outfits as a gimmick for their B and B. He understood they'd donned them first for another reason, though. Riley, Savannah, Nora and Avery had come to Westfield to escape a modern existence that was leaving them flat. They'd wanted to pursue creative goals their day jobs hadn't left time for. Wearing the Regency clothing was supposed to remind them on a daily basis why they'd come to Chance Creek—and keep them isolated from the outside world that could so easily intrude and dislodge them from their path.

They hadn't counted on how many other women loved the Regency time period—nor for their need to make money from the manor. They'd managed to combine their interests and need for cash into their B and B. They still had time for their creative pursuits, but they also had an income—and were sharing their love for all things Regency with other women, too. Of course, when the men had arrived, bringing Renata and her camera crews, any hope they'd had for privacy was gone. They'd taken it all in stride and didn't seem to mind being filmed anymore.

The show's audience loved it.

Still, compared to Addison's bikini and the flowy things she'd worn when she first arrived, the Regency getup was downright staid. Sure, it showed some cleavage, but not much else. If you'd asked him, he would have said he'd preferred the sexier clothing she'd worn off the plane, but there was something appealing about her now, too.

Something… intriguing.

It would be fun to get her out of that outfit, he decided, and he didn't realize he'd grinned until she grinned back at him, mischief lighting her eyes.

Did she want him to get her out of it—later, when they were alone?

"You look absolutely gorgeous," he said slowly, meaning it now that he'd taken a good look. "You look different, though. Not… flowy and bohemian. Dressed like that, you could almost be… sensible."

Hell. Should he have said that?

It wasn't very sexy.

Addison's eyes widened for a split second, and she half turned to look at the meal he was preparing on the counter as if to hide her reaction. "Do you need help?"

"You should probably get set up for the night first," Kai told her, afraid he'd hurt her feelings. He'd actually meant it as a compliment in a way. His mother would approve of her far more in this getup than in that bikini. "I guess—" He looked at the meal with frustration. "I guess I'll help you do that after I finish cooking." Maybe they'd get a minute alone and he could explain what he meant. Or better yet, skip that conversation altogether and get right to the part where he showed her he was attracted to her.

"When are you ever done cooking?" Curtis said with a laugh. "You want me to show you where to set up your tent, Addison? Otherwise it'll be midnight." He was obviously joking, and Kai knew he expected Addison to turn him down.

He did, too.

It was a shock when, after a pause, she glanced at the camera crew and said, "Uh… Yes."

Kai stiffened. So did Curtis. "Oh… okay," Curtis said. "Well, right this way." He shot an apologetic look at Kai before escorting her out into the main room of the bunkhouse. Addison didn't look back at him at all. Just hurried after Curtis. Several of the camera crew peeled off to follow them.

Kai wished they all had gone.

What the hell had just happened?

JUST WHEN SHE was getting somewhere with Kai, Curtis had to go and ruin it all with his stupid question. Of course she didn't want him to set up her tent. She wanted to do it with Kai.

But a question meant a yes.

Felicity was going to pay for this.

"Where do you want your tent to be?" Curtis asked, clearly as uncomfortable as she felt. They'd stopped by a storage shed and fetched the things she'd need, and he was carrying all of it.

"Here's fine," she said, pointing to the first empty space they came to in the makeshift campground by the bunkhouse. As she'd seen on the television show, four tiny houses had been built into a sloping hillside nearby. Those belonged to the married couples. As a singleton, she'd stay in a tent for now.

A breeze swooped through the campground, and Addison shivered. She hadn't thought too much about the sleeping arrangements—or about tenting. She hadn't done much of that since she'd been in scouting years ago. She hoped the sleeping bag Curtis had fetched would be warm enough tonight.

"Uh… that one's mine." He indicated a tent not three feet away. "Avery's the only woman here not married. Her tent is over there." He led the way.

Addison shook her head and followed him, aware of the stupid cameras that'd caught that whole exchange. Why hadn't the man told her where Avery camped before asking her to pick a place? Now it looked like she was trying to be close to him.

When they reached the women's area, she tried to help him set up the tent and only managed to get in his way. In the end she stood by, watching the cameras watch her as Curtis did it himself. Once it was up, he put down a pad and rolled out her bag for her.

"There you go. Nice and snug."

Now what was she supposed to do? "Thanks," she said. "That was... great." She was certainly no actor, and the longer she stood here, the more conscious of the cameras she became.

"My pleasure," Curtis said.

She waited a beat then stepped forward, just as Curtis did, too. They crashed together, and Curtis reached out to hold her up.

Addison yanked herself out of his arms. "I'll see you at dinner," she said desperately. Would the man never leave? She was sure her face was scarlet.

"Addison? Oh, good—you've got your tent up!"

Thank God, Addison thought as Avery hurried toward them, followed by Nora, Riley and Savannah. Curtis excused himself quickly, and Addison had to stop herself from flinging her arms around the women in thanks for rescuing her.

"We were about to have a meeting about some upcoming guests. Do you want to join us?" Savannah asked.

"Sure. We can talk about the ball, too."

Too late she realized she should have led up to that

a little more carefully. All the women stared at her. "Ball?" Riley asked.

Whoops.

"I told… I promised… Alice said…" She wasn't making sense. Best just to blurt it out. "I told Alice we'd host a ball at Westfield. A Halloween ball. A masquerade. In a couple of weeks."

"But—" Avery looked to the others.

"We've got a large group of guests arriving soon. And another group right after them. We wanted to leave a week free before your wedding," Riley told her. "If we throw a Halloween masquerade, we won't get a break at all."

"And you just got here—" Nora broke off when Riley sent her a pointed glance, but Addison knew exactly what she'd meant to say. She'd only arrived today, and she was planning balls?

"I'm so sorry; Alice was the one who brought it up, and she seemed to really want us to do it, and I… I got carried away." That wasn't true; Alice had forced her into it. What would happen if the rest of the people here figured out her predicament? Who knew what they'd ask her to do? "Look—" Desperation gave her a good idea. "I'll take care of everything. I'll need to learn the ropes from you ladies, but I swear the ball won't give any of you any extra work to do. I love putting on parties." That much was true.

Avery brightened. "You do?"

"Absolutely. I threw them all the time in Connecticut. Halloween is my specialty." She didn't mention her plan to become a professional event planner in New York.

"Well," Riley said, "if you'll handle the work, why not? We can open our doors to some of our friends."

"It would be nice to attend a ball without having to be the ones throwing it," Savannah added.

"I'm not sure that's realistic. Do you want to take on all that extra work by yourself?" Nora asked Addison.

Addison wasn't sure whether to laugh or cry. "Yes."

THE EVENING HAD gotten quite chilly, and Boone and Clay were building a large bonfire to keep everyone warm while they ate their dinners. Soon they'd have to bring meals inside for the winter, Kai thought as he prepped. The bunkhouse main room could hold them all, but it wouldn't be nearly as atmospheric as out here. He figured they'd do this as long as they could—but it wouldn't be much longer. Autumn brought rain in Montana, and they'd already had some wet evenings. Tonight looked dry, though.

He wondered how the rest of Addison's afternoon had gone. She hadn't returned to the kitchen, although Curtis had.

"Made a fool of myself," he muttered to Kai low enough for the camera crews not to hear. "Tripped and almost knocked Addison over."

"Let me guess—they got the whole thing," Kai said with a glance back at the cameras.

"You bet. Brace yourself; they'll make it look like I

went in for a kiss. I didn't," he said when Kai shot him a look, and he left the kitchen again, leaving Kai to wonder if that was true. Maybe Curtis wasn't over his lost bride at all. Maybe he'd wanted to be the next one to be married. He'd warned Kai that someone else might want his wife-to-be.

Had he been warning Kai about his own intentions?

Kai found that hard to believe, but the idea was like a scab he couldn't stop picking at as he worked on the meal. When Addison finally arrived in the kitchen, she seemed subdued, which only served to increase Kai's paranoia.

"Everything all right?" he asked.

"Yes," she said, then rolled her eyes. "But I did something stupid."

Kai stiffened. Had she kissed Curtis? Or wanted to?

"I let Alice Reed bully me into promising we'd throw a Halloween ball. Now Riley and the rest of them think I'm totally thoughtless for agreeing to it without even asking them. The only way to salvage the situation was promise to do it all myself."

"I'll help," Kai said, relieved more than he would admit this was the only thing troubling her. He was repaid by the look of gratitude she cast him. "But... a ball? Does that mean food?"

"I think so."

"Not a sit-down dinner," he said. Please, God—not that. A ball meant a crush of people, and that could easily deplete their stores.

"Avery says they usually do a buffet."

Hell. He didn't know what to think of that. Was the food supposed to come from Base Camp or from the B and B's supplies? Those were kept separate from the food for the inhabitants of the ranch. B and B customers weren't part of the game. But this wasn't a ball for B and B guests, so he wasn't sure where they stood.

When it was time to serve dinner, Kai wished he could hang back in the kitchen, but Fulsom and his people had arrived. Luckily there were only a few extra mouths to feed—not an entire entourage. He took his plate outside and sat near Addison, who was already devouring her meal as if she hadn't eaten all day.

"Everyone? Quiet down a minute. Martin Fulsom has a few things to say to us," Boone announced. "He flew in just an hour ago. Let's give him a round of applause."

Kai joined in with everyone else, and the silver-haired man bowed his head to accept their acclaim. Fulsom was in his fifties but fit as a fiddle. The kind of man who drew your attention no matter what he said or did. Kai knew this footage would appear on the next show. Fulsom waited until the applause died down, made sure the cameras were focused on him, spread his arms wide and began to speak.

"The easy part is over. Time to get to work," he boomed.

Kai straightened. There were murmurs throughout the assembled crowd. What did Fulsom think they'd been doing? Ever since they started Base Camp, it had been a race to beat the clock he'd set for them. Kai reminded himself that Fulsom was a showman. He liked to shock them. Kai resolved not to be shocked.

"Think about it," Fulsom told them. "Everything you've done up until now you need to keep doing. In the rain, the sleet, the snow and the freezing temperatures of a long Montana winter. In addition to that, you'll need to live off the food you've been setting aside for winter. I'm here to talk about details."

Kai couldn't help but feel uneasy, as if somehow someone might have leaked their shaky circumstances to the man, but everyone had sworn to keep the secret. Still, Fulsom was right; things were about to get more difficult.

"Housing," Fulsom said. "Brief me."

"We have all the housing sites dug except one," Boone answered quickly. "So we're all set on that. We hope to have four more tiny houses built before the really bad weather sets in."

"Seems to me you're cutting it close. What happens if you fail? These tents aren't going to be very comfortable when the snow starts to fall."

"Some people will have to sleep in the bunkhouse through the winter. I'm confident we can make that work and beat the housing deadline."

Fulsom nodded. "Food," he boomed. "Seems like this is where you'll fall down on your faces."

Kai swallowed down his worry the man was right. He wasn't sure who was going to answer Fulsom. Angus was studying his hands in his lap. Boone's jaw was tight as he looked away.

In the end it was Samantha who stood up. "We've got it under control," she said firmly. "We'll keep the greenhouses running through the winter growing hardy greens so we always have something fresh. We've got crops harvested and stored." Kai noticed she quickly moved on from that point, since the only stored crops left were the vegetables that had already been in the kitchen when their root cellar was raided. "We planted a crop of wheat last spring that is almost ready for harvest and have a contract with a local miller to turn it into flour. And if all else fails we have bison."

Kai admired Sam's quick thinking. She'd glossed right over the problem areas and concentrated on their strengths.

Fulsom considered her. "Wheat, huh? Seems to me your wheat should have been harvested already."

Kai shot a look at Renata. She was grinning, which made sense. Kai figured Fulsom knew little about wheat; Renata must have fed him that question to ask.

"You're right," Sam said. "We were late planting it, and we'll be late harvesting it, but so far, so good."

"Okay—we'll see how you're doing in a couple of months. I'd give you fifty-fifty odds that you all are begging to give me back the ranch around February. You ever see what scurvy does to people?"

"We won't get scurvy," Walker put in calmly. The large Native American was clearly unimpressed by Fulsom's threats. "Lived my whole life here—we can live off the land if we need to."

Kai appraised him. That was interesting. He hadn't

thought to ask Walker about that sort of thing.

"In February?" Fulsom pushed.

Walker nodded. Never a man of many words, he wasn't one to repeat himself.

"Wives!" Fulsom shouted suddenly. "Four down, six to go! Do you scruffy, ugly tree huggers really think you can score enough women to win this thing?"

Addison turned toward Kai, eyes wide, clearly insulted.

"Because if you don't, this land is going to become Chance Creek's first bona-fide suburb! You should see the seventy lovely homes Montague plans to build right here. They're amazing. All of them look *exactly the same*!" Fulsom was hamming it up for the cameras, but Kai couldn't take his eyes off Addison. She seemed to be working something out in her mind, but he couldn't fathom what until she leaned in close to him.

"That's for the show, right?" she finally whispered to him. "The whole thing about losing Base Camp? There isn't really a developer, is there?"

Kai pulled back. "Of course there is. Didn't you see the first episode?"

"Yes," she said hesitantly. "Montague. The guy with the steam roller?"

"Yeah, that's him. He's real, all right. He's desperate to build houses on this ranch; Fulsom's giving him the land if we screw up. That's why we're in such a rush to get everything done. That's why you're here," he reminded her. "You know that, right?"

Addison blinked, and Kai's stomach sank.

"Yes," she finally said.

IT WAS REAL. *Base Camp* was real.

And Addison didn't know what she was supposed to do now.

She'd only come here because Felicity had assured her it was fake. Now she was trapped. All these people she'd gotten to know today were betting their future on the outcome of this show. For the first time it sank in what they'd lose if Fulsom gave it to Montague. Kai was right; she'd seen episode one, and the threat that Montague would pave Base Camp over had added spice to the reality television show.

But it had only been a show.

Now she was wearing a Regency gown. She'd been in the manor. Seen the bison. Chatted with all the cast members.

Knew exactly how much this place meant to everyone.

What if she destroyed it all?

She'd stumbled into this silly show as a joke— hostage to Felicity's sick sense of humor. She never would have messed with people's futures the way she was now if she'd known the show was real.

Addison slipped away as soon as she could without arousing suspicion, made her way to one of the composting toilets set up around the camp in discreet positions and shut the door, yanking her phone from her pocket. Avery had informed her all the women shared a phone to cut down on distractions, but she hadn't put hers away yet.

Pick up, pick up, pick up, she willed at Felicity when she punched in her number. When her sister finally did, she launched right into her without a greeting.

"Felicity, it's real. It's all real, and if I don't marry Kai, the show is going to end. These people are going to lose their homes. What do I do?"

"Slow down, sis. I didn't catch any of that," her sister said, and Addison sucked in a breath. Felicity sounded strange. Her words were slurred. When she heard voices in the background, Addison realized Felicity had to be out with Evan. At a restaurant, maybe? Or a club.

And she was drinking.

Felicity never drank.

She wasn't like the models who managed their weight with prescription drugs; Felicity kept her figure through hard work and strict attention to caloric intake. She didn't like to waste her calories on alcohol, which was good. She didn't handle it well.

"Felicity? Are you all right?"

"Sure," Felicity said, although she sounded anything but. "Mom stopped by," she added. "Wanted to see why I kept turning down jobs. She noticed I was packing."

Uh-oh. Addison could just bet how that had gone.

"Once she stopped screaming, she told me I was smart to run away. No one would want to know me once I stopped working."

"She said that?" Addison was furious. "What is her

problem?"

"I'm her problem," Felicity said. "I'm being an ungrateful daughter. She made me a supermodel. She shouldn't have wasted her time. That's what she said, anyway."

Addison's eyes filled with tears at the pain in her sister's voice. "You know that's not true."

"It is true! I was five when I started all this. I wasn't the one shopping my photo around."

"Maybe she helped. That doesn't mean you wouldn't have made it without her. Honey, where's Evan?"

Right on cue, she heard a masculine voice in the background.

"I'm fine," she heard Felicity tell Evan. "I just don't know why you even want to be with me."

This was worse than Addison had thought. Felicity was losing it.

Evan came on the line. "Hey, Addison. Can Felicity call you back later?"

"Of course. Evan, take care of her, okay? She seems really upset."

"You know your mother." He sighed. "This is why we're going to Rome. You know that, right? Felicity is going to miss you like crazy. You'd better come visit."

"I will."

"I'm sure she'll call you back tomorrow. I'm going to get her home and put her to bed."

"Okay." Addison cut the call and put her phone away, wishing there was more she could do for Felicity.

There wasn't much she could do from Base Camp, though. She was grateful Evan had come into Felicity's life. He was a constant her sister could depend on, someone who truly believed in her.

Addison used the composting toilet, pulled herself together, washed her hands in the little sink set up outside equipped with cold water and natural soap, and returned to the fire pit. She was on her own; Felicity wasn't going to come to her rescue, so she'd have to sort this out herself. Fulsom was gone. Everyone else was talking amiably as the fire burned down. Kai must be in the kitchen, cleaning up from the meal.

Addison dithered as long as she could, but in the end she joined him there, grabbing a dish towel and drying the dishes as he washed them. For once, no camera crew was in there with him.

"You honestly didn't think any of this was real?" Kai asked after they'd worked in silence for several minutes.

"I did—but I didn't," she tried to explain, desperately wishing she hadn't said anything. She could have found out what she needed to know far more discreetly than blurting out her question. Now he'd be suspicious of everything she said and did. Which would make it hard for her to figure out a plan. "I thought you were doing everything I saw on television, but I thought it was scripted. That's what people told me about reality television."

"That's what *who* told you?"

"My sister. She's a model," Addison tried to explain.

"She has friends who do film stuff."

"That might be the way some shows are run, but not this one. There's enough drama going on all the time without it," he pointed out. "They kind of set it up that way."

"I guess so."

"So, you thought there'd be someone to tell you what to do?"

Suddenly Addison was exhausted. She wished she could climb into her tent and go to sleep—and wake up in the morning with a script in hand she could follow so she knew she was doing it all right.

She didn't want to think what this meant about her and Kai. Had he really invited her here to marry him? Was there a chance she could spend a lifetime with this man who took her breath away every time she went near him?

She couldn't believe that could be true. Didn't know what she'd do if it was. In the short time she'd been here, he'd already swept her off her feet, but that was when she'd been treating it like a fantasy.

Now it was... real.

"Yes."

"Today must have been quite a shock then."

"You could say that."

"What are you going to do now?" Kai kept scrubbing the dishes.

Addison wasn't fooled. She read the tension in every move he made.

She put a plate away in the cupboard and came back

for another one. "Wing it. I guess. Throw a Halloween ball. Try not to get in the way too much."

He softened. "You'll do fine."

"Will I?" she asked. "I'm not that good at winging it."

"Come on. Addison caps for surfers?" he reminded her.

"Yeah. Well, there's that." But she hadn't even come up with that; Felicity had. Felicity should be the one here, she realized. She had no doubt Kai would fall in love her sister if he met her.

Jealousy surged through her at the thought. She didn't want Kai to fall in love with her sister. She wanted him to want her.

As much as she wanted him.

Which meant she'd already gotten herself in a jam. Because Kai had fallen for the woman he thought she was—the woman Felicity had created, not the real Addison. She didn't knit surf caps, or prance around in wet bikinis, or dye her hair, or any of it. What would he think if he knew the real Addison?

Would she interest him at all?

"It's all kind of… overwhelming," she admitted.

"I bet it is." Kai straightened and dried his hands on a towel looped through the handle of the stove. She thought he'd lead the way out of the kitchen. But the dishes weren't done.

Instead, he moved to box her in against the kitchen counter, bracing one hand to either side of her.

Addison's breath caught.

"I'm sorry you're overwhelmed," he said. "But there's one thing I need to know right now. Because my future—and everyone else's here—is riding on it," he said.

Addison needed to stop him, but she was too late. He was already asking the one question she definitely couldn't answer.

Kai held her gaze, his face only inches from hers. "Addison, are you going to marry me?"

She swallowed. Fought for the courage to tell him the truth. She had to say no, because she hadn't come here to marry him, and marrying a stranger on a television show was plain crazy. And because she had dreams and aspirations that meant she needed to be in New York.

Kai waited as she fought for words, but all she could think about was the way they'd joked together while preparing lunch, the way he'd held her hand as they walked to the creek.

The way he'd kissed her.

And how badly she wanted to get to know this man better. How much she craved the touch of his hands on her skin.

She braced herself.

"Yes," she said.

CHAPTER SIX

S HE'D SAID SHE'D marry him. Addison had looked
him in the eye and said she'd marry him.

So why did he still feel so uncertain?

Maybe it was that despite her assertion, her earlier
question still nagged at him.

That's for the show, right? The whole thing about losing Base
Camp? There isn't really a developer, is there?"

If she'd thought the action on the show wasn't real,
why had she come? Did she simply want the experience
of being on television? What other reason could there
be?

What about the marriage aspect? She must have
thought their weddings were fake, too.

Which meant she hadn't come here to marry him at
all.

So why had she come?

They had finished the cleanup, and now Kai led the
way through the little campground as the sky darkened,
turning the question over in his mind. She must have
had a reason. After all, he was partially using *Base Camp*

as a way to leapfrog over the competition to launch his cooking show. What if she had a similar plan?

A knitting show?

Kai shook his head. That didn't seem likely.

Although who could account for taste.

"This is me," Addison said with a little flourish as she stopped in front of one of the tents in the women's section. He had the feeling she was eager to shake him. He wanted answers, though.

"Addison," he began.

"How am I supposed to get this outfit off?" she blurted. Kai remembered the way she'd deflected his questions earlier at the creek, and his suspicions grew.

"What do you mean?"

"This... corset," she leaned in to whisper with a glance at the cameras that had followed them. "You should see the way they tied it on me. I'm stuck."

"I can help with—" Kai bit off the rest of his words as reason asserted itself. For a moment the idea of undressing Addison had kicked his doubts to the curb. But he needed to be careful. He'd been well on the way to falling for her, thinking his luck had been too good to be true, but that was just it, wasn't it?

It had been too good to be true, and he needed to learn Addison's real reason for being here.

"Addison? Do you need help?"

Kai turned to find Riley approaching. To his frustration, she bustled over, making further conversation impossible. "I'll take it from here, Kai," she said. "Addison's had a long day. She probably needs some rest."

Realizing he'd been dismissed, Kai thought about digging in and waiting until he and Addison were alone again, but relief was plain to see on Addison's face. She did look tired—and the situation had to be overwhelming.

Maybe he was overthinking this. Maybe she'd come because she was attracted to him and had simply thought this would be a short-term affair. It didn't have to be anything more sinister than that. If that was the case, maybe he could still persuade her there could be something more between them.

As it was, he could only say, "Good night, Addison."

"Good night."

Did she look disappointed for a moment? Had she been hoping he'd stay? Undress her? Kiss her again?

Kai's blood, cooled by his doubts, heated again. But Addison turned to Riley. "Thanks for helping."

Kai made his way back the bunkhouse. He'd have to wait to get his answers.

He doubted he'd sleep tonight.

ADDISON KNEW KAI had wanted to ask her a lot more questions. He'd looked so shocked when she'd asked him if all of this was real, she now knew for sure it was. She could only imagine what he thought of her. From his perspective the question must have been a doozy. If she hadn't thought the show was true, why had she come to marry him?

When he'd walked her to her tent, she could see him turning the questions over in his mind, and she'd been grateful Riley had come when she did to prevent any more conversation between them. She had to talk to him about what was happening. But first she needed to figure out what she wanted to do.

She'd told him she'd marry him—which was a total lie. Which meant she needed to tell him she wouldn't. He really did need to find a wife—or risk losing his home. She couldn't ruin his chances—and everyone else's—to secure Westfield for good.

But telling him meant leaving Base Camp, just when she'd gotten here. She wasn't ready to leave yet. Everything about the place intrigued her, not least Kai Green. She wanted him to kiss her again, she admitted to herself.

She wanted a hell of a lot more than that.

Pushing those uncomfortable thoughts from her mind, she bent to unzip the tent flap, but Riley stopped her.

"Come to my house; it'll be easier there. Boone's not around."

She led the way to one of the tiny houses, and Addison forgot her worries as she stepped inside and gasped.

"Oh, it's beautiful, Riley."

She'd seen its interior on the show, but it was better in person. All done up in wood, handcrafted to be one-of-a-kind, the small house had an organic feel, like it had grown out of the ground rather than been built. Large windows lined the southern walls, and Addison figured they'd flood the house with light during the day. Riley moved to pull the drapes.

"Stand here and I'll get you undone," Riley said when she was finished.

Addison did so, still entranced by the house as Riley helped her out of her gown.

"These things can be a nuisance," Riley went on. "But they are awfully pretty."

"I love this dress. I can't wait for the ones Alice is bringing—"

Addison broke off, realizing she wouldn't be getting any more dresses. Not if she confessed to Kai she had to leave.

She was unprepared for the disappointment that coursed through her. She'd never have a tiny house, would she? Her life would seem so plain after this trip. Coming to Base Camp was about the most exciting thing she'd done in years. When she went to New York she tended to be a bystander to Felicity's life. She went to Felicity's parties, shopped where Felicity wanted to go. Hung out with Felicity's friends.

Here, she was taking center stage. It was a new feeling. A heady one—

But that's why she was doing this, wasn't it? So she could return to New York, take possession of Felicity's penthouse and create the exciting life she'd always wanted?

"You'll be amazed at how wonderful they'll be," Riley said. "When Alice makes a dress just for you, it's magical."

Magical.

Addison had always wanted a magical life, but if she left the show and went back to New York early, she'd lose any chance she had for that. She wouldn't get the penthouse, would have to scrounge around for a new job—

And she wouldn't have Kai…

"Everything okay?" Riley asked, stepping back so Addison could awkwardly pull her gown up and over her head. Riley got to work on the ties of her corset. "I know it's really overwhelming here at first. But you'll get used to it. Besides, there's Kai. He makes it worth it, doesn't he?"

"Yes," Addison said slowly and glanced over her shoulder. "But do you think… he likes me?" She still couldn't believe that could be true. If he didn't care for her, it would be so much easier to leave.

Riley chuckled softly. "Oh, he likes you. That's plain to see," she said.

Addison turned this surprising statement over in her mind. "You really think so?"

"You know what I've realized since I've been here?" Riley asked as Addison peeled off her corset and set it aside, dressed only in her shift now.

"What?"

"We make love so complicated, but it's not. It's actually simple. It's just a feeling in your gut, and you either have it or not. It can take time to grow, of course, but usually it's right there at the start, too, even if you don't want to acknowledge it. So, don't think; just ask your gut. Do you want Kai? Deep down? You don't have to tell me the answer." She smiled. "You can borrow my robe to wear back to your tent or to the bathrooms. Alice will provide one for you when she brings you the rest of your things." When Addison was wrapped in the light garment, still wearing her shift and underthings, too, Riley escorted her to the door. "Give yourself time before you make any decisions about Kai and Base Camp," she advised. "Do what your gut tells you, not your head."

"Okay." Addison hurried back to her tent, clothing in hand, swapped them for her toiletries bag, made a quick trip to the bunkhouse bathroom and soon was back zipped inside. When she'd folded her things as best she could, she slipped into her sleeping bag. The mat was thin, and the sleeping bag was warm but not nearly as comfortable as the bed she'd sold. She wondered if she'd sleep tonight.

She lay on her back, stared up at the nylon tent ceiling and thought about Riley's question.

Okay, gut, she asked herself silently. *Answer truthfully, putting all reason and caution aside. Is there any way I'd go through with this marriage?*

She didn't get an immediate answer; her mind was swamped with too many potential problems. What role could she play here? Sous chef? How did she feel about country living? Extreme country living. She was a city girl through and through.

Would she…?

This was ridiculous. Of course she couldn't marry

Kai. He was a stranger. A man with aspirations that didn't match her own.

A stab of disappointment had her rolling to one side. She curled up in her sleeping bag and forced herself to stay with the feeling. *What is it, gut?* she asked. *Do I want Kai?*

Her body responded immediately to this far simpler question with an intensity that made the answer impossible to refute.

Everything she'd ever imagined about Kai flooded her mind, her dreams made far more vivid by the details she'd gathered while spending a day with him. She'd been daydreaming about the man ever since she'd begun to watch *Base Camp*. She'd envisioned what it would be like to be with him. Pictured Kai's hands on her bare skin, his mouth on hers, his body poised between her thighs. She'd pictured him entering her…

Addison lurched up onto her elbow. Hello. Where had that… *lust*… come from? They'd only kissed.

And that kiss had made her weak in the knees.

Yeah, she wanted him.

You came here to win the penthouse—not to marry a Navy SEAL chef, she told herself.

But her body didn't care. It wanted Kai. Needed him.

Thought marrying him was a brilliant idea.

She lay down again, unwilling to succumb to such insanity. Maybe the real problem was the fact she'd been trying to win the penthouse at all. Maybe this was fate's sick way of showing her how presumptuous that was for someone like her. She wasn't the penthouse kind; she was a worker bee, not a queen.

Maybe she was supposed to get to New York under her own steam. Maybe she should forget about owning and resign herself to renting for the rest of her life. Find some little studio apartment she could afford. Find a new job and just keep working—

She'd have to commit to that plan, though. Be realistic about it in a way she hadn't been being about the penthouse. She'd never have been able to stay there long-term, after all. Why get used to luxury only to give it up again?

What would a realistic life in New York City look like? Who would be her friends there? What kind of neighborhood could she afford to live in? Would she even like it with Felicity gone?

She turned over again.

She could stay here.

Alone in her tent, the cold air creeping in until she tugged the sleeping bag up around her shoulders, Addison let herself think about that possibility seriously. If she stayed here and married Kai, what would she be saying yes to?

A community.

Shared work.

Fresh air.

Interesting people.

Kai.

Did she need a penthouse?

She sat up. Of course she needed a penthouse. It

had been her dream for years—ever since Felicity had gotten one. She loved being high up. The view. The windows. The star treatment from everyone. And she wanted the kind of business a person who lived in a penthouse would have. Celebrity clients. Red carpet parties.

But when she pictured herself striving for that—whether from a penthouse or a shoebox apartment—while Felicity and Evan lived in Europe, the vision seemed... empty. She'd always pictured life in New York with Felicity nearby. She'd wanted to re-create the fun they'd had as kids when pageants weren't involved.

Without Felicity—and Evan—she'd have to start all over if she moved to the city, and she wondered how it would feel to rattle around in a huge penthouse all by herself. Even if living there was free, she'd be on a shoestring budget, trying to start a business, scrounging for clients who didn't care she had no experience—

Was that any better than living in Hartford?

Suddenly unmoored, Addison found herself clutching the bedclothes.

And picturing Kai again.

No matter what the future held, she wanted to spend more time with him.

I don't have to make any decisions tonight, she decided firmly. She needed more time—more information.

One week, she told herself. She'd already left her life behind to take this challenge that Felicity had imposed on her. She'd keep saying yes for one more week. She'd let the universe do what it wanted with her. But at the end of that week, she'd use logic, foresight and her usual practical mindset to make up her mind what to do next.

Which probably meant she'd say no to Kai, no to Base Camp.

And no to New York City.

KAI'S QUESTIONS HAD kept him awake long into the night, and when Addison turned up in the kitchen early the next morning, she didn't look like she'd fared much better, but she was brisk and cheerful as she entered the room, and when she asked how she could help, he didn't turn her away.

Maybe he was overthinking this. She'd asked about scripts and she was right; many reality television shows did run that way. She might have been concerned about winging her way through the filming. It was reasonable.

She'd said she'd marry him, he told himself again. He should be content with that.

But he was anything but content.

The day had dawned bright, one of those blue-sky fall days with a nip in the air that was bracing rather than uncomfortable. Kai pulled out his notebook, flipped it open and showed her the recipe for a breakfast hash he'd long ago memorized how to make. He knew later he'd need to meet with Angus and figure out what else they needed to do to bolster their dwindling supplies. He'd make sure Addison was somewhere else. He couldn't trust her with this secret.

And that killed him, because he wanted to. He wondered what ideas Addison would have about the predicament they found themselves in. She wasn't a gardener, he reminded himself, but she was creative. You never knew.

Addison bent over the book, looking at the recipe he'd written in it, the notes all around it in his neat block printing and the tiny sketches he'd made in the margins: potatoes, a grater and other ingredients and tools used to make the dish.

"This is so… cool," she said. She flipped a page or two. "There must be hundreds of recipes in here!"

"At least three hundred," he admitted. He felt a little strange about her leafing through the book, like someone was looking through his diary—which he'd never kept, for the record.

"All these notes. Why are there all these different sets of cooking times?"

"Conventional oven, convection oven, solar oven on a sunny day, solar oven on a cloudy day."

"Do solar ovens work on cloudy days?" she looked up, all curiosity.

"Not all that well," he admitted.

"And the rest of this stuff. How to find the ingredients locally… notes about growing things… this is a treasure trove. Do you have a backup copy? Please tell me you have a backup copy," she said sternly.

"Nope." He'd never thought about a backup copy. "This is the only one."

"It should be under lock and key," she exclaimed.

He couldn't help the pride that welled up in his chest. He forgot all his troubles for a moment. She got it. He wasn't sure anyone else except maybe Boone understood the scope of his work. Kai took a moment to look at her again.

Hell, she was beautiful. Dressed in the same Regency gown she'd worn the day before, she was neat and trim, sweet but sexy.

Delicious.

"You should publish this," she went on, back to leafing through it again.

He scoffed. "No one would be interested. But I'm trying for a cooking show." Kai snapped his mouth shut. Why on earth had he told her that? He didn't know if he could trust her yet. "No one else knows," he said quickly. "Except Renata." So far no one had noticed the extra crews filming him, or if they had they must have thought it was because he was the next to be married.

She nodded solemnly. "I won't spill the beans," she promised. "You'll be a shoe-in for that, though. You're an amazing cook, and you know how to explain things. Plus, you're hot; women will love the show. And you're a SEAL, so men will get into it, too."

He was hot? Kai hadn't heard anything she said after that. Addison thought he was hot?

Desire stirred in him. He thought she was pretty hot, too. Despite his doubts, he itched to touch her.

"Kai, this is all so amazing," she went on. "How will you make it happen?"

"I'm already in touch with a producer. I'm waiting to hear back from him about cutting a pilot." He couldn't help himself. "Do you really think it will be a success?"

She beamed at him. "Yes."

OVER THE NEXT two days, Addison threw herself into the goings-on at Base Camp. If she was taking one week out of her usual life, she'd decided it was all or nothing. She'd never get this chance again. When she left the show early she'd need to restore her career back in Connecticut—or find a way to move to New York on her own without going broke. She'd have to work, work, work… just like she'd been doing. She had to make the most of her time here.

First off, she'd decided she wanted to know everything about Kai—and everyone else at Base Camp. If she had to leave in a week, she wanted a lifetime of memories from the experience.

She'd decided to start with the women, who were about to contend with a large party of guests. She sat in on several meetings and soon got the lay of the land at the bed-and-breakfast. There were a number of activities the women did with all their guests, starting with fittings for their very own Regency clothing. Alice Reed took care of that, having premade gowns ready to alter quickly to fit the guests, like the one Addison was wearing now. Next it was carriage rides, Regency dance lessons, watercolor painting lessons and lavish meals. Once she got a feel for the basic itineraries, it was easy to see where she could help. She used every spare minute she had to relieve the other women of preparation and cleaning duties so they had more time for their personal pursuits.

For her part, Addison loved every part of it. Alice brought her more clothing, and even cleaning was fun in her still new Regency work dresses as she got to know every corner of the beautiful manor. Preparing for the guests' arrival had been even better. Nothing made her happier than company.

She knew many women dreaded housework, but she'd always taken to it. Cleaning stood for more than wiping away dirt to her. It stood for a feeling that a guest got when he or she walked into your home. It stood for her intentions toward her company; her intentions toward her own life. When she spiffed up a room she felt she was opening herself up to possibilities. Creating magic. Setting a stage. The guests had arrived last night, and Addison was doing everything she could to help.

When she could, she worked on the costume ball, too, determined no one else would suffer for her sins. She refused to let herself think about the fact she wouldn't be there to experience it. She'd already realized one thing all the women at Westfield had in common was their determination to come through for each other in a pinch. If she left before the dance—no, *when* she left, Addison corrected herself—Riley or Avery or someone would step in and make sure it came off just fine.

First came the invitations. Addison wasn't going to add any expenses to the women's budget, so she went to town with the Russells and bought invitation blanks on a lovely, heavy paper, paid for them herself and, after creating a guest list with Riley's help, used calligraphy to address them by hand.

She was pleased with the results. Calligraphy was another of her talents—and hobbies. She didn't get to use it enough. The handwriting made the invitations seem more old-fashioned, too. In line with a costume ball held at a Regency B and B.

She'd talked to Felicity, who apparently didn't even remember Addison's call the night she'd been drinking. Addison decided to keep her concerns to herself. Instead of telling her again that everything on the show was real, she asked for Felicity's help for the props she needed to make the ball a success. "You owe me," she said. "It's your turn to say yes."

Her sister had, willingly.

Knowing that Felicity had the decorations well in hand, Addison turned to the question of music, and Maud Russell helped her there, too. She'd heard all about the ball from Alice, and she begged Addison to leave the music to her. "We know such wonderful musicians. We'll take care of everything."

Addison accepted gladly, wondering why Alice should go to such trouble when she was the one who'd imposed the ball on Addison to begin with. Maybe she felt guilty. Rightly so, Addison thought, although she couldn't stay angry with Alice. The ball was going to be fantastic.

It killed her she wouldn't be there to enjoy it.

Once more cautioning herself to stay in the moment, a mantra she'd always derided but now was her lifeline, Addison focused next on food and drink, but it turned out Maud was all over that, as well. "My cook, Mrs. Wood, will be happy to consult with you."

"Mrs. Wood is a dream," Riley told her when Addison questioned this arrangement. "Just let her run with it unless you have specifics in mind."

"Who does the shopping?" Addison asked her.

"No one. The food magically appears. I'm serious," Riley said when Addison laughed. "The Russells end up underwriting so much of our parties it's awful. But you can't stop them. Believe me; I've tried. They're like, gazillionaires. I have no idea where they got their money, but they spend like there's no tomorrow."

When Mrs. Wood, a sweet, industrious woman, got in touch with her, Addison had several requests, but she quickly realized the other woman knew far better than she how to prepare for a ball.

"You aren't upset, are you?" Addison asked Kai later that night. They had fallen into a pattern of taking a walk after their work was done. They talked over their day, Addison carefully steering the conversation away from any discussion of the future. Sometimes they kissed. Kai never pushed things further than that; after all, they were being filmed. "You're the chef here. Maybe you want to be in charge?"

"Hell, no. I mean, if I was in the kitchen, I wouldn't get to have any fun. I want to dance with you."

"You do?" Addison was surprised. She hadn't

thought Kai would enjoy that, but when Kai took her hand and pulled her close, she let him. He swung her around in a waltz. He was light on his feet, masterful at guiding her.

"Yeah, I do." And he kissed her. "We'd better figure out our costumes. We need to match, right?"

"I guess," she said, flustered when he backed away. She wouldn't be here to wear a costume. "I… uh… don't know what I want to be," she said to cover her confusion.

"How about I be Anthony and you can be Cleopatra. A toga is pretty simple."

Addison immediately saw the possibilities, but she shut down her enthusiasm. She wouldn't be attending the ball, she reminded herself. "Yes," she said softly, suddenly wishing things were different. "But we'll get Alice involved. No bedsheets." No sense embarrassing Kai, even if she wouldn't be there to see him.

"I don't actually have any bedsheets—all I've got is a sleeping bag."

CHAPTER SEVEN

KAI WAS PEELING potatoes from their dwindling supply the next morning when his phone buzzed in his pocket. Addison was chopping onions, scraping the pieces into a big metal bowl every so often. He had to admit he was getting to like having a prep cook. It sped things up, and Addison was easy to work with.

It had been hard to let her go to her tent last night after their walk. Kissing her was torture since he couldn't do more than that with the camera crews around.

Waiting was killing him, but these were early days. He didn't want to rush things with Addison.

"Kai here."

"Hold for David Linkley."

David Linkley? Kai nearly dropped the phone in his attempt to juggle it on his shoulder while wiping his hands, stripping off the apron tied around his waist and smoothing a hand over his hair, as if the producer could see he wasn't camera-ready at the moment.

Which was ironic, since he was being filmed even

now.

Addison, head cocked, raised an eyebrow. Kai turned his back on her.

"Kai?" a masculine voice boomed over the line.

"Yes. David?" Crap. Was he supposed to call the producer David? Had he ruined his chances in his first utterance?

"David Linkley here. Want to talk to you about this cooking show idea you've got."

"Great." God, he sounded like a boys choir drop-out, his voice cracking and weird. He had to pull it together.

"*A SEAL's Meals*. I love it. It'll sell great with the barbecue crowd. The armchair quarterbacks who like to get their friends together to watch the game. That kind of thing."

"Uh—" Barbecue crowd didn't sound right at all. Kai cooked everything, but he didn't serve up slabs of meat as a rule because of the damage to the environment that came from the overgrazing of cattle. He'd envisioned aiming his show at a younger, active, educated crowd who loved eating—but were environmentally conscious, too.

"We want to shoot a pilot. At Base Camp."

All Kai's concerns flew straight out the window. David Linkley wanted to shoot a pilot?

"That's... great." Fuck. What was he saying? Didn't he know any other words?

"Good, good. Glad you're on board. I've talked to Renata. She's all for this. It's going to be complicated, though; film crews filming film crews. Very meta. Very now. Don't you worry, we'll make this show shine. All you have to do is show up with your star power. Think you can do that?"

"Great. I mean—yes. Yes, I can do that. I'll be ready for you."

"We'll send over particulars when we have them. Renata will fill you in on our ideas."

"Gr—that sounds terrific. Can't wait to work with you."

Linkley hung up, and Kai turned around and pumped his fists. "I got a show!"

"You got a show?" Addison dropped her knife on the counter and rushed to him. Kai swooped her up and spun her around.

"I got a show! We're filming a pilot right here!"

"When?"

"I don't know. Soon."

"That's fantastic!"

"I know. Isn't it great?" Kai set her on her feet, wrapped his fingers in her hair, tilted her head back and kissed her square on the mouth, not caring if they were filmed, not stopping for a long time, either. This new victory had fired him up even more, and the hunger he'd felt earlier increased to a gnawing pain. When could he be alone with Addison? When would it be all right to pursue a closer connection? Kai fought for control. When he finally pulled back, he had to steady her. "Sorry; got carried away. You all right?"

She grinned at him. "Yes."

Kai's phone buzzed again. "Hold that thought." It was Grace. "I've got to take this. Sorry." He answered the call. "Grace! You won't believe this!"

"How's the wife thing going?"

"Good. Really good! But I got a television show!"

"I know; I've been watching it." Grace laughed.

"No—a new one. A chance at one, anyway. I'm filming the pilot soon." He explained everything to her, noticing that Addison was listening in, beaming at his excitement.

"That's terrific! Everything's coming together, isn't it?" Grace said.

Something in her voice stopped him. "Yeah, it is. You okay?"

"I am. Too okay. Kai—I'm scared."

He clutched the phone, ready to spring into action at a moment's notice. His elation disappeared in a flash. "What's going on. Are you safe? Where are you?"

Addison's smile faded, and concern furrowed her brow.

"Kai—it's not like that. I'm fine," Grace assured him.

"Then what's happening?"

"I'm being a freak; that's what's happening. Everything's good. My work is good. My life is good. My fiancé is good. We're buying a house, Kai. A little place near Mom and Dad. They're helping us with the down payment. It's small, and it needs lots of work, but it's perfect."

"So, what's wrong?" He had begun to pace the

room. Addison watched him, leaning against the counter, her work forgotten.

"Nothing. That's what's wrong; there's always something wrong. When's the other boot going to drop?"

Kai took a deep breath. He understood what she meant. Even after all their years with the Ledbetters, they still expected life to fall to pieces at any moment. "Maybe it's not. Maybe this is how life is now. Try to soak it in while you can. You know there's always going to be some little problem to solve. With your job and a new husband and a house to fix up? There's bound to be hiccups, but they don't have to be bad ones anymore."

"You think so?" Grace's voice had gone thready, and Kai wished he could give his sister a bear hug.

"Yeah, I think so."

"What about you?"

"Things are pretty great here, too." He nodded at Addison, who relaxed and nodded back. She turned to the vegetables she was preparing.

"Are you soaking it up?"

"Trying to." Kai laughed, watching Addison work. "Yeah, I'm really trying to."

"There'll be things for you to solve, too," Grace said.

"Bound to be."

"But today's good, huh?" she asked softly.

"Yeah, today's good. Let's hold on to that."

"Okay. Thanks. I'm happy for you, Kai."

"I'm happy for you, too."

THE NEXT MORNING, Addison woke with a pit in her stomach. Two days left until her self-imposed deadline to leave Chance Creek, and the thought of it made her want to curl in a ball and hide under the covers. She'd already grown comfortable with the rhythm of her life here at Base Camp. Each day, she did a half hour of prep work and another half hour of cleanup around each meal, helping Kai. In between, she went up to the manor with the other women and pitched in there, taking over most of the daily chores, freeing up the other women to see to their guests. As soon as she'd realized Samantha worked in the gardens, Addison had told her not to worry about pitching in at the manor anymore. Kai had mentioned it was harvest time and that they were scrambling to store enough food for the winter. Addison wanted to do all she could to help. He always seemed strained when he talked about the harvest.

She hated to think she was going to let them all down in just a few days.

As for leaving Kai…

She wasn't sure whether to be grateful or furious he hadn't tried to take their relationship to a deeper level. Her time with him and the kisses they'd shared were going to make it nearly impossible for her to go when the time came. If she slept with him—

Addison shook her head to dislodge that thought. She hadn't slept with him. And she wasn't going to. She realized now that would be unfair to them both. There was no way a single time with Kai would quench her thirst for this man. As hard as it was for her to believe, she was coming to think he might feel similarly about her. Although, that was an illusion. He still thought she was the woman Felicity had made her seem in her video. He didn't know anything about her, really.

It was best to keep things simple. Easy to break off.

Addison snorted. Yeah, easy.

She sat up and climbed out of her sleeping bag, suddenly anxious to hold on to every moment of this day so she had something to remember when she got back home to her empty life—

Addison froze.

Empty life?

"Addison?" a feminine voice whispered outside her tent. "Are you awake?"

She was grateful for Avery's interruption, because she didn't want to unpack the meaning of that phrase. She wasn't going back to an empty life; she was going back to the chance to pursue a long-held dream.

At least, she hoped she was. If Felicity decided to be a stickler for the rules, she was really going back to a nonexistent actuarial job and a nonexistent apartment in Hartford. Or to a hole-in-the-wall apartment in New York City where she'd have to take whatever job came her way, for now.

"I'm here," she whispered back. "Hold on; I'll be right out." When guests stayed at the manor, the women took turns sleeping up there to be on call during the night. Addison had gotten used to the fact that it took help to get in and out of her Regency gowns, so she was glad the others always made sure someone was in Base Camp. Avery was an early riser, so this wasn't the first time they'd assisted each other.

She welcomed Avery's whispered chatter as they walked to the bunkhouse, where they took turns showering and primping in the bathroom. By the time they were dressed there was a lineup for the single inside shower, but Addison knew Kai and some of the other men would use the outdoor ones, even in this cool weather. She wasn't nearly that tough, although the thought of Kai naked and lathered up was intriguing.

She found herself watching Kai as they prepped for breakfast, all too aware that in just a few days she'd be gone and wouldn't ever be this near him again. She'd never guessed this would become so painful. If Felicity had wanted to shake her up, she'd done a good job.

Avery met her at the manor door later that morning with a fistful of RSVPs for the ball. "It's going to be the event of the season."

Her words hit Addison like a fist to the gut. The event of the season.

And she wasn't going to be there.

What was she doing leaving all of this behind? Could she really go back to New York—or Connecticut—and make a life half this good?

Addison was torn. On the one hand, she was enjoying herself so much here. She had built-in friends, engaging work, a man who took her breath away.

On the other hand, this was a ranch in Montana—and it would always be a ranch in Montana. She could throw a hundred balls and there wouldn't be any red carpets or paparazzi. Her events wouldn't be written up in the society pages. And Kai was no millionaire—

"Addison? Are you okay?" Avery touched her arm, concern written in her face. "Come to the kitchen. Let's get you a cup of tea."

Addison followed her automatically, her mind wheeling. Paparazzi? Society pages. A millionaire? Was that what she was after?

Who was she trying to be... Felicity?

She sat down hard in the chair Avery pulled out for her in the kitchen and took the cup of tea when Avery placed it in her hands. She was grateful no camera crews had followed her here.

Because it occurred to her that's exactly what she'd been doing for years; waiting for an opportunity to become Felicity. And that was—awful.

It wasn't true, she decided. Not really.

She didn't want to her sister's relationship with their mother. Didn't secretly have a thing for Evan. Didn't want to be a model.

But she wanted the glamour, the attention, the self-confidence... the penthouse.

And she'd been putting off moving forward with her own life out of fear she couldn't attain any of that.

She groaned. "What am I doing?"

Avery looked at her in alarm. "I don't know. What are you doing? Are you having second thoughts about

Kai?"

Addison shook her head. About Kai? No.

About herself. About the way she was wasting her life. She'd been waiting for a fairy godmother to come and change her into someone like her sister. That was never going to happen, though. Even if she attained her dream and became a fantastic event planner, she'd never have Felicity's life.

She had to make her own.

She didn't even know where to begin.

Except…

Addison looked around. Here she was in a manor kitchen, in a Regency gown, on a sustainable ranch, participating in a reality television show in which she was supposed to marry her dream man.

Maybe she should begin right here.

"I just… I don't know what I'm supposed to…"

"Breathe," Avery told her. "Just breathe a moment." She demonstrated, and Addison tried to follow her cues. She was dizzy. Her head swimming.

Why had she ever wanted Felicity's life anyway?

It wasn't like she hated herself. She had her own work. Her own hobbies. Her parties. She loved her parties. She'd never done those to be like Felicity. She did them out of love.

"I'm good at throwing parties," she said aloud.

Avery nodded. "I can tell. You really love working on the ball."

"I do. But—" Could she say it out loud? Would Avery understand? "I've been going off course. Trying not to be me. Trying to be someone else."

Avery nodded again. "Who do you want to be?"

"I don't know." She hated feeling so unsure.

"But you know you like parties," Avery said, and a smile quirked her lips. "I'm not trying to be sarcastic. It's something to hold on to. What else do you think you like?"

Addison was more grateful than she could say that Avery hadn't run the minute she started talking nonsense. It was as if Avery understood where she was coming from. Her practical questions were helping.

"I like this." Addison gestured to their surroundings. "I like being here. Having people to talk to all the time. Live-in friends," she added shyly.

"It's pretty awesome, isn't it?" Avery agreed.

Addison swallowed past the lump in her throat. "I love the manor. And I love Base Camp, too." She realized it was true; she loved the rough, camping-style camaraderie she'd found there. "I love being with everyone. And—" She broke off, not sure if she should go on.

"And?" Avery prompted.

"I like Kai," Addison whispered. "A lot."

"Sounds like you're exactly where you're meant to be," Avery said.

Addison found herself blinking back tears. "But I'm not in the right place at all. I'm supposed to—" She snapped her mouth shut and buried her head in her hands.

"You're supposed to what?" Avery leaned forward

and touched her arm, suddenly serious. "What are you supposed to do, Addison? Did Montague send you to mess things up?"

Shocked, Addison's tears dried up. "No. Of course not."

"But you didn't come here to marry Kai, did you?"

Addison bit her lip. Now she'd really blown it, and Avery was going to hate her; everyone would. She slowly shook her head. "I thought it was all fake," she said helplessly.

"Fake? You mean the show?" Avery dropped her hand and leaned back. "But then—" Her eyes grew wide. "You thought you were coming to play a part? Are you an actress?"

"No. It was my sister's idea. Because of this stupid book I was reading." Addison realized there was nothing for it except to explain the whole thing, so she did, starting with the day Felicity came up with the idea of the month of yes. Avery, to her credit, listened to her without comment. When Addison was done, she sat quietly, as if considering what to say.

"What should I do?" Addison asked her when she couldn't take it anymore.

"I think you should keep saying yes."

Addison blinked. "But—"

"You just told me you love it here, you love the work, you love the company, the manor, Base Camp—and Kai."

"I didn't say I loved him."

"You said you like him. A lot."

"There's a difference."

"Is there?"

"I've known him five days!" Addison realized she was twisting the fabric of her dress in her fingers. She let it go and tried to smooth out the wrinkles.

"Which is why you need to stay until you really get to know him. He might be the love of your life," Avery argued.

"But if he isn't, he won't have time to find someone else."

"Don't underestimate Boone," Avery said darkly. "He'll marry Kai off whether it's to you or someone else. Why not take a chance and see if it should be you? I can tell Kai wants it to be. Addison, you should see the way he looks at you. He's fallen for you, hard. Don't you owe it to him to see if you could love him back?"

"I promised myself I'd leave in one week. That it was the right thing to do."

"Well, I'm telling you it's the wrong thing to do. You need to stay here through the ball, at the very least. You can't leave us all in the lurch when you said you'd take care of it. One more week. Then, if you still want to go back to New York, Kai will have more than a week to find your replacement."

Addison winced. Her replacement?

Avery smiled. "See? You'd better stay, hadn't you?"

"I guess so." Avery was right; she had said she'd run the ball, and no matter how she tried to convince herself otherwise, she had fallen for Kai.

"Then it's settled. You're staying through Halloween. I won't tell anyone what you told me until you let me know what your decision is after the ball. But Addison—try to love him, okay? We need you."

Addison nodded. She wouldn't have to try. She was halfway there already.

"Go wash your face, and when you come back we'll get to work," Avery said gently.

"Okay."

Avery caught her hand as she walked by. "You're meant to be here; you'll see."

After freshening up, Addison forcibly turned her attention to her chores, refusing to acknowledge her relief at gaining a week's reprieve from leaving Kai. She and Avery talked over her plans for the event until Mrs. Wood arrived to finalize the menu and the B and B guests began to appear for breakfast.

When they were done, Maud and James Russell came by to pick up Mrs. Wood and insisted on taking Addison for a short drive.

"How are the preparations coming?" Maud asked when they were rattling down the lane. Addison loved the slow pace of the carriage and the way it made it seem they had all the time in the world to get where they were going.

"Quite well, thank you," Addison told her.

Maud fixed her with a sharp, knowing look and pronounced, "You are a party person. I recognize you because James and I are, too. There's nothing we enjoy more than planning a party."

"We like to make people happy," James put in, turning around on his high seat from where he held the horses' reins.

"But sometimes people make it so hard," Maud said. "Even Avery and her friends here at the manor. They don't want to take advantage of us."

"They don't let us take advantage of them, either," James said. "All these potential party guests, and we're banned from throwing parties."

"Not all the time, you understand," Maud said. "But we have to plan them carefully."

"We count weeks on the calendar, you know," James added. "Tricky business. Not the way parties are supposed to be at all."

"We confuse them by varying the type of get-togethers we hold," Maud said. "Dinner parties, dances, musical evenings…" She counted on her fingertips.

"But they catch on." James frowned.

"They invite us back." Maud steepled her fingers. "Very tiresome, this business of tit-for-tat entertaining."

"You see, it isn't the same."

"Oh, it's very nice at Westfield, don't you know," Maud hurried to explain, "and I enjoy being feted now and then as much as anyone, but—"

She broke off, apparently at a loss for words. Addison hadn't thought that was possible.

"But you see," James continued for her, "we like to be the ones *giving* the parties."

"I completely understand." Pleased to finally get a word into the conversation, Addison made the most of it. "Tell you what. As long as I'm here, I'll do what I can to make them accept."

"Splendid!" Maud and James seemed very happy, and Addison had to smile. She knew the Russells could help her make events at Westfield extraordinary.

Unless she went home.

"My dear," Maud said. "You seem made for Westfield. Are you happy here?"

"Yes," Addison told her truthfully, and she wondered again if she should stay for good.

MORNINGS WERE FAR better for birdwatching than afternoons, but as desperate as Kai was to spend some time with Addison, he'd take any excuse he could get. Breakfast and lunch came far too close together for him to have much time to spare mid-morning. As they washed and dried dishes from the noon-day meal, Kai asked casually, "Can you spare an hour when we're done?"

"Uh…"

At first Kai thought she'd say no. He knew how busy she was helping with the chores at the manor and preparing for the Halloween masquerade ball as well.

"Yes," she said.

He'd noticed she did her best to be accommodating. In fact, Kai thought as he scrubbed at a particularly encrusted pan, he wasn't sure if he'd ever heard her say no.

Funny.

"Is something happening I should know about?" she interrupted his musings.

"Just want to spend some time with my future wife," he said lightly.

"Okay." She turned away, which made Kai wonder—again—what her thoughts about marriage really were. They'd gotten stuck in a holding pattern in which they spent a lot of time together prepping and cleaning up from meals but never talked about the future.

At first Kai had wanted to give Addison time to settle into the reality of the show. If she'd come thinking the setup was fake, then he needed to give her a chance to adjust her ideas. When he'd asked her to make a commitment to staying, she had. But not convincingly enough. Something wasn't right, and it was time for them to take the conversation deeper. He had to know if she was going to marry him.

Kai blamed the presence of the cameras for their lack of real communication, which was why he'd asked Curtis to try to organize a distraction. He needed time alone with Addison if their relationship was going to progress.

When they were done with the post-meal cleanup, Kai led the way outside. Addison followed, and after her came the camera crew, who angled around to try to get ahead of them so they weren't filming their backs.

Curtis, still sitting at the fire pit with Angus and Jericho, leaped to his feet and shouted, "Holy shit!" pointing at the distant line of trees. He took off running, Daisy yipping and barking at his heels. Angus and Jericho followed.

The camera crew peeled off after them.

"Come on." Kai grabbed Addison's hand and began to run as well, but in the opposite direction. He made a quick stop at his tent and grabbed a pack he'd prepared, slung it over his shoulder and dashed with her down the track toward Pittance Creek. Halfway there, he steered them off and raced through the trees parallel to the running water. He knew a camera crew would eventually look for them at the creek where the track connected to it, but he also knew the crew members weren't particularly adventurous. They wouldn't bushwhack through the woods to find them.

When they were out of sight of the others, he slowed to a walk, suddenly conscious Addison was fighting to breathe. She wasn't dressed for jogging.

"You okay?"

"Give me a minute."

"I forgot about your corset."

"No wonder women used to faint all the time," Addison said, but her breathing was slowing and she smiled.

He took her arm and began to walk at a leisurely pace along the side of the creek until they'd reached an area far from where Base Camp's inhabitants usually strayed.

She waited for him to open his pack, pull out a blanket and spread it on the ground. "Are you going to explain that headlong dash?"

"No cameras," he said simply.

She raised an eyebrow. Was she wondering if he planned to seduce her?

He hoped to, but slowly. He didn't expect her to make love to him today. Despite the impression she'd given on first arriving at Base Camp, Kai had learned Addison wasn't impetuous. She thought through her decisions, and he had a feeling she'd take her time with a man before offering herself to him. He wouldn't have expected that from a woman who knit surf caps.

He wouldn't mind speeding things up, though. He had so much desire pent up his frustration made it hard to think these days. When she bent to take a seat on the blanket, Addison's breasts plumped up and it was all he could do not to reach out to trace a finger along the neckline of her dress. He'd like nothing better than to get naked with her and become acquainted with her body.

Instead, he handed her a pair of binoculars, and she took them with a bemused smile as he pulled another pair out of his backpack for himself.

"We're looking for *cyanocitta stellari*. Stellar's Jays," he explained, giving the common name. "And anything else we happen to see. I've got my notebook." He pulled that out, too. "Maybe we can add something to my list."

He sat down and patted the blanket beside him. A moment later, Addison joined him, taking off her bonnet and smoothing the long skirts of her Regency gown out around her.

They lay on their backs, and he showed her how to work the dials to focus the lenses, enjoying the excuse to touch her hands. They were small and shapely. Delicate yet strong. Just like Addison. He squashed the urge to lift one to his lips in an old-fashioned gesture. He didn't want to spook her even if they'd kissed before.

He knew Addison watched him when she thought she could get away with it. Knew she enjoyed their kisses. He wished he could get inside her brain and know what she was thinking right now. Where did she go in her mind when she grew quiet?

"I can see the treetops so clearly. I never thought to just look up with a pair of binoculars before."

"Look at the moon sometime," he told her.

"I'd like that."

Kai scanned the treetops with his binoculars, content to let the quiet forest, the beautiful day and the pleasant activity do their work. When he spotted a black-capped chickadee on a branch some distance away, he helped Addison focus on it, too. It was a common bird, one he'd seen dozens of times, but he shared Addison's joy in spying on something alive in its home territory. As time passed, they spotted several other species, as well.

"When did you get interested in bird-watching?" Addison asked, tucked beside him, her head resting on his shoulder. He'd put his arm around her when they'd focused on a nuthatch and he hadn't removed it. Addison seemed comfortable enough, and if his arm was threatening to go numb, it was a small price to pay for the closeness they were sharing.

"When I started surfing, actually. Waterbirds were my gateway drug. Really had a thing for pelicans for a while there."

"Pelicans, huh?"

"Got to be careful; they'll drag you right off your board if you're not careful," he quipped.

"You're making that up."

"Maybe."

"Not much chance of spotting a pelican around here."

"No."

"Do you miss California?" she asked, turning her head to look at him.

"No. Not really. I'm too involved with what we're doing here. What about you? Is it going to be hard to leave Connecticut behind?"

"Not Connecticut."

He waited. That hadn't sounded like the end of a sentence.

"I guess I always had it in my mind I'd live in Manhattan someday."

Kai held perfectly still, somehow aware that this was a crucial piece of information. She'd wanted to live in the city. Instead here she was in Montana, joining a sustainable community by volunteering to marry a stranger.

Like so much about Addison, it didn't add up.

Kai thought about his own roundabout path to Chance Creek. His decision to join the Navy because of a desire to protect people. His decision to become a SEAL—as if becoming some sort of superman would help him stop anyone else from feeling pain.

The SEALs had made him the man he was today, but while he was proud of the work he'd done with them, the experience had opened his eyes to how many children in this big world were at risk. Now he was approaching the problem from a different angle here at Base Camp. Trying to get a message out about food security. Hoping one day to have a bigger platform and the ability to write books, manuals and teaching resources.

He wished he could help create a world where no child would ever end up hungry.

His stomach tightened, a knee-jerk reaction that never went away when he thought of his past. He crushed the memories that sprung into his mind: waiting for the apartment door to open. For his mother to come home. Keeping Grace inside. Watching the food in the cupboards dwindle.

Then run out.

Kai swallowed, determined to clear the thoughts from his mind, and knew it was time to broach the question he'd brought Addison here to ask, but when he turned to Addison, her slow breathing tickled his face. She had fallen asleep, and he didn't have the heart to wake her. She'd been working as hard as any of them these past few days.

Kai took the opportunity to drink in the sight of her. Addison had already changed him. Made him more aware of everything around him. Things were different when she was near. He felt more hopeful. He liked the idea of having someone to share his future with.

It was like everything he needed was here in his arms. Tenderness rose within him as he watched Addison sleep. She was precious, and he wished he could tell her that. He couldn't get enough of looking at her. He wanted—

He wanted to make her his wife.

Kai sucked in a breath and let it out again. The feeling had crept up on him. It was different from the infatuations he'd experienced before. He could see himself creating a life with Addison. Aging alongside her.

Starting a family.

His thoughts had never progressed that far with another woman.

He must have moved, because when he looked again, Addison was looking back at him.

"Did I fall asleep?"

He nodded.

"I'm sorry."

"Don't be." He was glad she didn't try to get up. He wanted to stay here. Like this. For as long as they were able. Preserve the moment before something interfered with it.

He touched her cheek. "You needed a rest."

"I guess I did."

"Either that or I bored you with birds."

"You didn't bore me with birds," she said with a smile. "I like birds. I like looking for them—with you."

"Can I kiss you?" he asked.

Her yes was buried against his mouth as he made his

move, and Kai sighed inwardly, grateful for all the events that had led them both to this blanket on this piece of ground. The Universe had definitely gotten this right. When he slid his hand down to her hip and inched her closer, she came willingly, wriggling forward until they were pressed together, both of them lying on their sides.

"You feel good," she confessed when they came up for air.

"So do you." So good. It had been far too long since he'd had a woman in his life. Living like a monk wasn't his style, but as soon as he'd come to Base Camp and started being filmed, he knew that anything he did could make or break his future. Now he wanted to toss all that caution to the wind. And why not? He didn't have much time to get himself to the altar.

He took a chance, moved his hand and caressed Addison's shapely bottom through the fabric of her dress. She didn't pull back. In fact, she moved even closer to him.

That was all the answer he needed. She felt the attraction, too, and if he wasn't mistaken, she wanted him to act on it.

But this dress…

Kai pulled back and examined it with a frown. "How do I get this thing off?"

"Honestly? It's a pain in the ass. And we don't have a lot of time, do we?" She got up on her knees and turned around. "Just undo those ties back there and loosen the neckline."

Kai did so, and Addison tugged at her dress, fished inside the neckline—

And lifted her breasts free of the fabric of her chemise.

She looked up. "I really hope this is what you were angling for. If not, I'm going to put these girls away and leave on the next plane out of Chance Creek."

"This is exactly what I was angling for," he told her. Moving to kneel in front of her, he skimmed both hands up over her waist and higher until he cupped her breasts. "Has anyone ever told you you're beautiful, Addison Jones?"

She didn't answer that, but her breath caught when he slid his thumbs over her nipples and bent down to taste her. Addison closed her eyes and arched back to give him better access, and for the next few minutes he devoted all his attention to making her feel good. She was easy to please, and her soft sighs brought his body to full attention.

She lifted her hands to the top button of his shirt, and when she'd succeeded in undoing all of them, he pulled her into a rough embrace, loving the feel of her breasts against his chest. Soon he laid her back on the blanket, ducked under her skirt and went exploring.

"Kai—oh," Addison said when his kisses trailed up her thighs to the sweet spot between her legs. He peeled down her panties, got out of her way so she could get them off and came back to enjoy her even more. Judging by the sounds she made, Addison was all too happy to let him. She was soft, open to him, trusting him so completely it turned him on even more.

"Kai, I want you," Addison said some minutes later, and he didn't need to be told twice. He kicked off his boots, pants and boxer briefs, knelt between her legs and nearly came undone when she reached out and took the length of him in her hand. Braced there, it was his turn to close his eyes and give in to her ministrations. Her soft but firm touch soon had him in a desperate way.

When he couldn't hold on any longer, he kneed her thighs farther apart, pushed her dress up to her waist, eased into position and nudged against her. He let his eyes do the questioning. Watched her for her answer.

"Yes," she said.

He still hesitated. "Protection?"

"I'm on the Pill. Kai—" She put her hands on his hips and tugged him closer.

Pushing into her felt like coming home, and it took every ounce of his concentration to pull back and push in again. Addison was so hot. So sweet. So thoroughly with him as he stroked inside her. They found their rhythm, a strong pace of lifted hips and deep thrusts that soon had them both breathing hard. Determined to ride her all the way to an orgasm, Kai kept hold of himself, kept hold of his rhythm and worked in and out of her until Addison leaned back and gave a cry.

That unashamed sound of pleasure pulled him right over with her and they came together, his guttural grunts mixing with her sexy cries until they both collapsed in exhaustion.

Kai wrapped his arms around her, still inside of Addison, wanting to prolong the closeness. She clung to him just as tightly, even when her breathing slowed.

"I'm crushing you," he said finally and pulled out, rolling to one side, bringing her with him. Her eyes were luminous, and he thought he saw an echo of the joy she'd brought to him there. "What?" he asked. "What are you thinking?"

"I want to do it again."

ADDISON HAD NEVER felt like this after lovemaking. Energized. Charged up rather than depleted. Her body ached to feel Kai inside her again.

"Again? Like… now?"

"Yes." She loved saying it freely; not because of Felicity's rules. She didn't feel shy or embarrassed about what her body needed when she was with Kai. She refused to think about what the future might bring. Right now, this was all she wanted.

"I could go for that."

His answer was humorous, but she thought she heard wonder in his voice. Was he realizing—as she was—that maybe he'd found someone so compatible that lovemaking, like everything else they did, was easy?

She rolled away from him, flipped her skirts up and got on her hands and knees. Kai needed no more encouragement. In a flash he was behind her, hard again, bumping up against her in a way that made her buzz with desire to feel him inside her again. Hooking an arm around her, he had perfect access to her breasts, too. He tested the weight of them in his hand and groaned.

"God, you are so sexy."

She sighed as he played with her breasts with one hand and dipped his other between her legs, teasing her until she arched and moaned, the wonderful sensations nearly overwhelming her.

The only warning that he was about to enter her was the way he shifted behind her suddenly. Then he lodged between her legs and slid slowly in.

Addison gasped, feeling the length of him—and the girth—more acutely from this angle. His slow strokes, combined with the way he was still playing with her breasts, soon had her panting, pressing back against him. Wanting more.

Needing more.

She needed Kai, she realized. She had no idea what that meant for her plans—or for his. She'd never meant to come to Montana. Couldn't imagine a life away from the East Coast. Didn't know—

But, oh, being with him felt so good.

Kai increased the pace of his thrusts, and Addison clutched the rough blanket between her fingers, giving herself up to the sensations he was bringing to life. As he moved behind her, working in and out, the heat inside her flared to an irresistible flame. She couldn't believe the way he made her feel. Couldn't stop this if she'd wanted to; her body wanted Kai. Needed him. Craved the friction he was creating inside her.

She lost control just moments before he did, and

they came together a second time, the sensations rolling through her in waves until she finally collapsed facedown on the blanket. Kai pulled out a final time and turned her over to gather her into the protection of his arms.

"I'm not letting you go," he whispered into her hair. "You hear me, Addison? I need you."

She knew what he meant. She didn't want to let go, either. But staying meant taking a flying leap into a future she'd never planned for. How did you change your plans midstream?

But how could she leave Chance Creek and live—

Without Kai?

CHAPTER EIGHT

A S THEY DRESSED and made their way slowly back to the bunkhouse, Kai once more wished he could read Addison's mind. She held his hand tightly, as if trying to keep the connection between them, but her face was a study of worry and doubt that sent his stomach sinking.

Together, they'd been amazing. Moving into a rhythm so easily. Bringing each other such pleasure without any awkwardness or missteps. What had her so worried?

Was it because they'd known each other for such a short time?

Addison was a mess of contradictions. Sometimes she seemed so free and easy. Sometimes so caught up in her concerns. He wished he knew everything about her so he could guess what she'd do next.

"Are you okay?" he finally asked when they were nearing the camp.

"Yeah." She kept her gaze on the ground in front of them. "Yeah, I think so."

"You don't sound too sure." He stopped, and she did, too. "What's wrong? Are you regretting—?"

"No!"

Kai hesitated. He'd never heard her say that before.

"No," Addison repeated. "It's not that at all. It's just... do I... do I fit here?"

"Of course you fit here." Couldn't she see that?

"In what way?"

Kai bit back a curse. He shouldn't have to explain it. "We just made love—twice."

Addison's brows came together. "I don't mean with you. I mean here—at Base Camp."

"Isn't it the same thing?"

"No."

The ground dropped out beneath his feet, and Kai fought to regain his balance. Just a few minutes ago he'd been at the top of the world, convinced he'd found the one woman he could share his life with. And now she was questioning if she even belonged here at all?

"Why did you even come here?" He didn't mean to sound so angry, but this was his life they were talking about. More than that—

His heart.

She turned away, and Kai pursued her.

"Addison. Why the hell did you apply to be my wife when you thought the whole thing was a joke?"

"I... I don't know."

"That's not good enough."

"it's just... I wanted a different life."

Okay, he could understand that. Kai tried to calm

down. "And now you're wondering if it's the right life? Is that it?"

She turned to face him. "Yes. It's all moving so fast, and it's different than I thought it would be, and you're asking me to make a huge decision after a couple of days."

"You've been here a week and a half!"

Addison's eyebrows shot up, and she quickly bit her lip. Kai's jaw tightened. Was she—was she laughing at him?

He replayed the words he'd said in his mind. Found his own lips quirking.

Hell. A week and a half.

"Okay, that's not a lot of time," he conceded. "But you knew when you applied those were the terms."

"Except I thought it wasn't real," she reminded him. "Now I know it is. I have to be sure."

"You let me make love to you." He moved closer to her again.

"And it was wonderful."

He set his hands on her waist, willing her to know that was the most important thing. "When will you know?"

"Soon. I promise."

"I'm going to hold you to that."

He bent down and kissed her again.

IT WAS A long time before they stopped kissing and continued back to the bunkhouse. When Addison's phone rang, she swiftly pulled it out, grateful for the interruption. It was her parents' number, however, and Addison hesitated before taking the call. She hadn't told them anything about this trip, except to say she was traveling to see a friend. She knew her parents would have all kinds of questions if they knew she'd quit her job, left her apartment and gone to hang out with a strange man on a television show. Luckily, they'd never been fans of *Base Camp*.

"Hi, Mom," she said brightly, waving Kai on.

"Meet you in the kitchen," he told her, and she nodded.

"Addison Elena Reynolds!" her mother cried. "I cannot believe you. What do you think you're doing?"

"Uh…" What did her mother think she was doing?

"Don't bother to lie. I just watched this week's episode of *Base Camp*—because one of my friends informed me you were on it. Imagine my humiliation when I watched my daughter parade her body in front of a million people and prostitute herself to an actor? Did you give one thought to your sister or me when launched yourself into this venture?"

"Felicity—"

"Is so heartbroken she can't even answer the phone," her mother shouted. "Her career is already on the ropes. She's nearly washed up, hasn't had a job in weeks, she's running away to Rome to hide from it all and now you've done this!"

"Mom—"

"I can't believe you're defending yourself. It's jealousy, isn't it? You were always jealous of your sister.

Always wanted what she had. Never could content yourself with your limitations—"

"Felicity's the one who got me on the show," Addison burst out. "And she's not answering the phone because she's sick of you always clinging to her. You're the one who doesn't have a career. You're the one who's jealous of Felicity. Go get your own life, Mom." She cut the call and threw her phone into the trees.

Then spent five minutes finding it buried in a pile of dead leaves.

This was a mess, she told herself. Her mother was right; it was jealousy of Felicity's life that had gotten her here. Now it was time to choose her own path. One that really made sense.

She paced the track, trying to sort her thoughts. If she stayed, her days would be filled with a multitude of tasks. Helping Kai feed the people of Base Camp. Working at the bed-and-breakfast. Taking charge of some of the events—or maybe lots of them. She could lift the burden of much of the work that went into the Regency weekends from her new friends' shoulders, which they'd already proved they were grateful for.

Maybe she could expand their repertoire, too. Cater to larger events for companies. They already offered weddings. She imagined those were fun to prepare for.

She'd be surrounded by smart, creative people with a common goal. She'd have an opportunity to learn all kinds of things.

The only thing missing was the glitz and glamour of city life. Could she live without that? Could she give up the idea of cosmopolitan existence and make do with a ranch life, instead?

If she didn't—if she returned to Connecticut or New York—would she be happier?

One thing she knew: she didn't want to make her mother's mistake and try to glean happiness from someone else's leavings. Her mother hovered around Felicity the way Addison did when she attended one of her sister's parties. Off to the side, expendable. No one came to those parties to see her. They only accepted her for Felicity's sake.

The same went for her mother. She wasn't necessary to Felicity's career—hadn't been since Felicity was a teenager. She was superfluous, too.

Addison shook her head. That wasn't the life she wanted.

It wasn't the glamour and glitz she was after, either. She didn't need bling to make her happy. It was the details of her work that charmed her. The perfectly placed rose. The thoughtful gift. The right song playing in the background.

She could do all that here.

With Kai.

Addison's heart throbbed. That was the most important part of the equation: here, she'd be with Kai. There, she'd be alone.

When she put it that way, there wasn't any question what she'd choose.

Addison pocketed her phone and strode toward the bunkhouse.

She was ready to tell Kai what she'd decided.

Ready to tell him she'd stay.

KAI SLOWED TO a stop when he entered the kitchen and found Samantha and Angus there. Sam spent most of her time outside in the gardens. A cheerful, active woman, he was surprised to find her in her present state: her eyes rimmed with red, her arms crossed tightly over her chest. Angus looked grim, too. He shook his head when their gazes met.

"What's wrong?" Kai asked.

"The wheat crop," Samantha said. "It's not doing well. I think we're losing it."

Hell. If the wheat failed—after the potatoes and the rest of the root crops—

They'd be living on bison after all.

Not exactly sustainable.

"Are you sure?" Kai asked. He'd checked it just a couple of days ago. It had seemed fine then.

"I'm sure."

Angus nodded, too. "It's bad. I don't know if it got too much water or not enough, or if it's some kind of disease, or if we simply planted it too late last spring. Everyone else has harvested theirs. That's the thing; none of us knows what we're doing here."

"We knew there'd be a learning curve." Still, this lesson was really going to hurt. "How about the potatoes?"

"Too early to tell," Sam said. "They're an experiment. What if they don't make it?"

She was panicking, Kai realized, and he understood why. There was a lot of pressure on the food production team. The men and women working on the houses had a deadline to beat, too, but were well on their way to achieving it. Jericho's team had hooked up multiple power sources to run Base Camp on.

Now it was down to food. It was up to him to rally the troops. He was one step removed from the day-to-day operation of the gardens, which gave him the distance to see things more clearly.

"One way or another we're going to do this, and we're going to teach people about food security along the way," he told them. "We've got bison coming out of our ears. Eggs, too. We've got pork. Milk products. We're growing greens. And in a pinch Walker will use his foraging skills to get us through. Maybe we're going about this all wrong," he added. "Keeping our problems a secret."

Angus opened his mouth to protest, but Kai cut him off. "This is the kind of lesson we need people to learn. How to get by when it all goes to shit. Right?"

Sam nodded slowly. "You're right. If we pretend that nothing ever went wrong, other people won't learn how to problem solve when something does."

"You want to tell Renata about the root cellar and wheat—today?" Angus asked. He looked tired. Kai knew he'd been on guard duty last night. All the men were working on too little sleep.

"I think we should. We should explain our mistakes. Ask for help to solve them." Kai made a face. He wasn't looking forward to that.

"I'll do that," Angus told him. "You're not even a principal member of the growing team. We're the ones who should take the blame."

"I don't think this is about blame. It should be about solutions," Kai insisted. "That's the story. Let's note down everything we're doing to fix this. When Renata gets back, we'll spin the story our way. Then we won't have to sneak around to guard our food, either. We can be open about it—and about napping when we need to."

"Sounds good," Angus said reluctantly.

"How is it going with Addison?" Sam asked. "Are you two on track? Will you marry in time?"

"Yes," Kai said forcibly, but he wished he was as confident as he sounded.

ADDISON FELT FOR Kai as he faced off with Renata a half hour later. She was frustrated she hadn't gotten a chance to talk to him alone before he and Angus had called a meeting, but now most of the members of Base Camp had assembled in the bunkhouse on folding chairs brought out for the occasion. Only a few of the women had stayed with their guests up at the manor, where Riley was treating them to a watercolor painting lesson. The garden crew stood together up front. Renata confronted them, hands on hips.

"Someone stole all of your stored vegetables and you didn't think to tell me?" she asked again. "We could have framed a whole episode around that!" She shook her head. "Maybe it will happen again."

"Definitely not," Angus said. "We've posted guards and locked the root cellar."

"Without telling me." Renata looked fit to burst. Addison exchanged a glance with Avery. She understood Renata's anger, but she also understood why Kai and the others had tried to hide it from the director.

"It's going to be a long winter without vegetables," Avery whispered to her.

Addison nodded. "But they're already trying to grow more."

Nora stood up, and a cameraman focused on her slim figure. "We're low on fresh vegetables," she said. "Our meat supply is fine, though, right?"

"The problem is the wheat crop is failing," Samantha explained. "We think we can grow greens over the winter in the greenhouses. We're less positive about other vegetables just because none of us have tried it before. We're trying to get potatoes growing so we have something starchy."

"What about the canned goods?" Nora asked. "Don't we have enough of those to see us through?"

Angus, Boone and Samantha turned to Kai. "I hadn't even thought of those," Boone said.

"That's because there aren't any," Kai admitted.

Addison straightened. That seemed like an oversight.

"But…" Samantha stared at him. "What have you been doing with the harvest? We had tons of tomatoes and cucumbers…"

"We've been eating them. I thought we'd have plenty of fresh winter vegetables to see us through," Kai told her. "Why eat canned stuff if you can have fresh?"

"That's… ridiculous!"

It was the first time Addison had seen her angry, and Avery seemed startled, too. Normally, Sam was a cheerful woman with a ready smile.

"We trusted you to plan our food use. You said that was your thing. How could you just not can anything when you had bushels of food to preserve for the winter?"

"It wouldn't have made any difference. If we had any canned food we would have stored it in the root cellar, too."

"You didn't know the cellar would be broken into. Not canning anything is criminal! Why—?"

"I hate canned food!" Kai burst out. "All right? That's not the way I do things. I eat with the seasons. The plan was to feed you fresh food year-round, not some disgusting leftovers from the back of a cupboard." He shoved a chair aside as he strode across the room and out the door, slamming it behind him.

Silence reigned in the bunkhouse until Addison jumped to her feet and followed him, bursting out of the door to find him well on the way down the track toward the creek.

"Kai," she called, then picked up her skirts and raced after him. "Kai!"

He didn't slow down, even when she caught up to him. Addison strode alongside him. "None of this is your fault."

"Yes, it is," he said heavily. "Samantha's right. I could have canned enough to keep us in vegetables all year round. I might have stored some of that food in the bunkhouse, and we'd be in a much better place. Instead I made soup after soup, salad after salad, stir-fry after stir-fry, and now look at us."

"The others made an assumption. They could have canned the food as easily as you—"

"It was a smart assumption—that the person in charge of the food would can a few jars."

"Why do you hate canned food so much?" Addison asked.

Kai slowed down a little, and she was grateful. It was hard to keep up with him. "I'm adopted," he said suddenly.

"Adopted?" She fought to keep up. What did that have to do with anything?

"My mother—she wasn't ready for kids. She had my sister Grace and me when she was a teenager. She'd left home. She was always bouncing back and forth between friends and boyfriends. We didn't have a home of our own until I was seven." He walked on a ways. "Hell, she was so proud of it."

His pace slowed again, and Addison held her breath. She'd had no idea Kai had a childhood like that. When they'd spoke of their families, his parents had seemed so normal.

"She finally got a steady job as a waitress. When she showed us our new place, we thought it was a palace.

Grace and I got the bedroom. My mother slept on the couch. It came furnished—with a television. The utilities were included." He chuckled grimly. "That was crucial."

"I bet." Addison wanted to touch him, but she was afraid to interrupt. She had a feeling it was important for him to tell her this.

"What we didn't realize until we got there was if Mom was working, it meant we had to stay home alone. That had never happened before; we'd always lived with other people."

"Alone? At seven?"

"Seven and four," he corrected. "It was my job to watch my sister. My mom worked evening shifts. She'd lock us in. We weren't supposed to open the door under any circumstances except a fire. We had to be quiet so no one knew we were there."

"Kai." Addison's heart ached for the little boy he once had been. "That was a lot for you to take on."

He nodded. "Not in the best part of town, either. You can imagine what we heard. We always kept the television playing on low to block it out. To keep the dark away. Mom's shifts ended around two or three in the morning. I could never sleep until she got home, but once she did I'd crash, and everything would be okay. Then one day she didn't come home until the following afternoon."

A chill raced through Addison's veins. "What happened?"

"She said she had a double shift. Said as long as we

kept inside everything would be fine. Not to worry. It was just work." A muscle tensed in his jaw as he swallowed. "I have never been so scared in my life."

Addison's heart squeezed. She could only imagine what that admission cost him.

"It got worse," he said. "She started having double shifts all the time. Sometimes it was two or three days before she came home. I learned how to cook mac and cheese. I'd hold my breath when I heard footsteps in the hall. Hope it was her, dread that it wouldn't be. I had to keep Grace from talking too loud, keep the television turned low."

"That's not okay. What was she thinking?"

"She wasn't. My mom was an addict. I didn't understand that back then. Now I do." They'd reached the banks of Pittance Creek, and Kai stopped. "She wasn't at work all those extra nights; she was turning tricks. Getting high. Coming home when she couldn't score anymore. One day she didn't come home at all."

Addison waited, knowing there was more to come.

"We waited, like usual. I watched Grace. Kept her quiet. Kept the TV playing. We ate the mac and cheese. The crackers. The cereal. Then we ate the canned soup. The canned chili. The canned green beans. Black beans. Fava beans. Finally tried a can of sardines. We didn't like them much."

A tear spilled down Addison's cheek.

"She didn't come home. And there was nothing left. I don't know how many days she was gone. I broke the rules—" Kai's voice cracked, and Addison longed to pull him into her arms. "I opened the door—just to see if she was coming. Someone saw me."

He paced away suddenly, his fists clenched by his sides. "They called Child Protective Services."

"Thank God."

He swung around, and the anguish on his face struck Addison dumb. "I was supposed to wait," he told her. "If I'd just held in there—"

"You could have died," Addison cried. "Grace could have died. What your mother did was wrong!"

"We got scooped up, put in foster care. They found my mom. Tried to get her into a program. She could have had us back."

"Jesus!" Anger coursed through Addison. "She didn't deserve you back!"

"She was my mother." Addison watched him pull himself under control. "She was my mother. But she didn't want us back. She said they could keep us. When the Ledbetters asked to adopt us, she signed us over just like that."

"Because she knew she couldn't raise you," Addison said. "Not because you opened the door."

He opened his mouth to say something, lifted his hands and suddenly strode away.

This time Addison didn't pursue him. She knew a man like Kai wasn't going to succumb to emotion where she could see him. She knew he needed a chance to let those feelings out. She hugged her arms to her chest as a chill wind sprang up, lifting leaves to dance in billowing circles. She watched one land in the creek and slide away.

How the past could haunt a person, she mused. How one small action—one short sentence—could change a life. Kai had opened a door. She'd closed a figurative one once in her life and always wondered what would have happened if she hadn't. Fate had turned a corner, and life had marched on. Neither of them could guess where they'd be today if they'd chosen differently.

The thing was, she wanted to be right here, Addison realized. Here with Kai, ready to listen to him, talk to him, hold him—whatever he needed once he'd confronted his pain on his own.

She turned when footsteps approached, surprised to see him coming back.

"I don't want to walk away from this—from you," he said simply. "I don't want to be like her."

"You're not. And Kai—you yourself said she was young. An addict. I think—I think at some point you're going to have to forgive her." She closed her eyes. "Wow. I'm a hypocrite. Forget it—don't listen to me. I don't know what I'm talking about."

He took her hand and waited for her to open her eyes again. "Why are you a hypocrite? Do you owe someone forgiveness?"

Addison wasn't sure. "She's still doing it," she began, then started over. "My mother. And it's such a small thing it doesn't bear mentioning after what you've said."

"Let me be the judge of that."

She had a feeling he was relieved they weren't talking about his past anymore. Maybe she should push him to talk more, but instinctively she knew he'd said enough for one day. They'd revisit it another time, when his emotions weren't so raw. Maybe it would be kind to distract him with her far more petty problems. Although they weren't petty to Felicity. She was moving halfway across the world to make a change.

"I began competing in beauty pageants before Felicity was even born," she said. They'd reached the creek, and she sat down on the bank. Kai sat down beside her. "My mother loved dressing me up for them, teaching me to sing, all that primping and fussing."

"Did you like it?"

"I liked the attention—especially all the attention I got from her. It was something we did together. I was a bit of a show-off. Liked to belt out a tune."

He chuckled, and she was grateful to see he'd relaxed.

"Then Felicity joined in. I wasn't as pleased with that. At first, she was in the baby categories, and that was okay, but when we got a little older, it became very clear Felicity was pageant gold. And I wasn't."

"That must have hurt."

"I stuck it out for a while. I'd get third place now and then. Felicity won every category every time. And Mom focused on her." Addison shrugged. "Which makes perfect sense."

"But not to a little girl." Kai was frowning now. He took her hand and rubbed his thumb over her knuckles.

"Not to a little girl," she echoed. "One day I'd had enough. I confronted her. Said maybe I should just quit—"

Addison swallowed, unprepared for how sharp her pain still was when she thought of it.

Kai's lips pinched together. "Let me guess; she agreed with you?"

Addison nodded. "It hurt. Bad. My dad stepped in. Did his best. Got me into sports. I actually went to school on a softball scholarship at first. Injured my arm and that was that."

Kai touched her arm. "I didn't know."

"It's fine for everyday life. Just not for throwing fastballs." She stared at the water. "I let those old pageants make me feel second best, and that's not fair to me or Felicity. I'm glad I came here. I don't think I'd ever really have realized how much I was living in the past if I hadn't."

"How about your sister?"

"Felicity? She's a supermodel now. Has a beautiful penthouse in New York City. A wonderful husband. But my mother—" Addison shook her head. "It's like she's trying to suck the lifeblood out of her. She's so obsessed with Felicity's career. My sister is moving to Rome." Tears pricked her eyes. "I'm going to miss her so much."

"She's moving to break free from your mom?"

"Yes. Don't get me wrong; she loves Mom. We both do. She's not a monster."

"She's just not operating with your best interests at

heart."

"I think Felicity and I both wonder if we're lovable." She'd never put it so starkly, and saying it took her breath away, but it was freeing, too. It explained so much.

Kai cupped her chin and turned her to look at him. "Yes, you are. I can guarantee that."

When he kissed her, something shifted inside Addison, as if a giant boulder slid away from her heart so there was room to let him in. She clung to him, suddenly needing him close.

"You are lovable, Addison Jones," Kai said when he pulled back. "And I want to marry you. For real. Not because of the show. Not because of anything except I want to spend my life with you. Would you... be my wife?"

Once again Addison pictured herself on the edge of a cliff—Kai down below waiting to catch her. This time Felicity wasn't pushing her. She was on her own. She had to make her own decision.

It was surprisingly easy. In her mind, Addison stepped back, took a deep breath and seized a running head start.

Leaped off the cliff into the abyss—

"Yes."

CHAPTER NINE

WHAT A DIFFERENCE a day made, Kai thought as he and Addison worked in tandem to get breakfast ready for everyone else the following morning. The rest of the camp was so tense you'd have thought they were in danger of imminent starvation, while he and Addison were cocooned in a bubble of mutual love.

She'd said yes. Kai still couldn't believe it. He knew their time by the creek last night would stand out in his mind as one of the moments that changed everything. Life with Addison would be different from anything he'd ever experienced. He'd have a true ally, a woman of integrity by his side.

They'd had to return to camp soon after his proposal, and when they did they found the meeting had broken up.

"Everyone's cranky, but we'll be okay," Boone said when Kai caught up with him. Kai wondered if Boone, too, blamed him for not canning part of their harvest, but he was the kind of man who looked forward, not back.

All Kai could do was look forward, too. He'd apologize when people had simmered down, but for now all his attention was taken by Addison. When he'd joined her in her tent last night, they'd made love then whispered plans about their future until the wee hours.

Today, he found every excuse he could to touch her. He couldn't believe she was real.

She was his.

The meal was a quick one, with only the men and Sam eating it. The rest of the women, except Addison, were seeing off their guests at the manor.

Kai and Addison were working on the dishes when his phone buzzed in his pocket. He wiped his hands on a towel and pulled it out. "Hello?"

"Hold for David Linkley."

David Linkley. This should be interesting.

Kai leaned against the counter. This time he wasn't half as nervous as he'd been the last time he'd talked to the producer.

"Kai—how's Montana treating you?" Linkley boomed when he came on the line.

"Just fine. How are you?" He was pleased to note he was handling this far better than his last conversation.

"Good, excellent. Just letting you know I'll be sending some paperwork your way. We want to get this thing rolling. Next week sound good for you?"

"Of course."

"Now, a couple of details. First of all, we've changed the name of the show. *A SEAL's Meals* is just a little... well... childish, we thought. We're going with

Feed Your Army. What do you say about that?"

"Uh... I served in the Navy," Kai pointed out.

"We thought of that, tested out a few different versions, but let's cut to the chase—our test audience didn't score Navy as high as Army. Army sounds wholesome. Active. Navy—well, there are connotations."

Was he serious? Kai had a sinking feeling he was.

"But, sir, I can't go on a show and pretend I was in the Army—"

"Of course not. We won't be talking about your military history in anything but a general way. Don't want to upset anyone or make the show political. You know what I mean."

Kai wasn't at all sure what he meant. Sustainability was a political topic no matter how you sliced it. He didn't care if he offended anyone—

"We're going to make this a family show. Something Dad will relate to. Barbecue. Hearty fare. Good ol' hamburgers, meatloaf. That kind of thing."

"I don't use a lot of beef in my cooking," Kai told him. "We can talk about bison, but like I tried to tell you last time, my philosophy of food—"

"Kai, let's get one thing straight here." Linkley's voice changed. "Your philosophy of food is whatever our biggest sponsor tells you it is, and that sponsor is going to be the beef industry, so don't tell me you don't cook with beef." Linkley let that sink in. "I think you'll find that show business is a team industry. You know how to be a team player, don't you, Green?"

"Uh… yes, sir." He'd spent thirteen years in the service being a team player.

This was different, though.

"I'll send that paperwork over, and you get it back to me ASAP, you hear? We'll get this ball rolling and get you on your way to being a star. What do you say about that?"

"Uh… that sounds great, sir."

Great.

He was back to sounding like an idiot. Feeling like one, too, he thought as he cut the call and pocketed the phone.

"What was that about?" Addison asked, tugging at the side of her dress. It was the second time he'd seen her do that, and normally he'd ask what was the matter, but not now.

"Selling out to the man. Be back later. I need some air."

ADDISON PREPARED TO head up to the manor, not taking Kai's sudden departure personally. He'd obviously gotten some disappointing news. She hoped his show hadn't been cancelled, but by the sound of things that wasn't the issue. Instead, it sounded like that big-shot director was trying to push Kai around.

Kai didn't strike her as the type to put up with that for the most part, but everyone did strange things where their dreams were concerned. She'd talk it through with him later. She was due at the manor to help clean up after the guests who had departed. Besides, she desperately needed to find Riley or someone else who could help her retie her corset. Riley had done it this morning and tugged it one jerk too tight, but she'd asked if it was all right, and Addison, stupidly, had said yes, even if there wasn't a camera filming her. She'd gotten so used to the automatic answer, and she was paying for it dearly.

Now her corset was cutting into her side with every move she made. She'd been about to ask Kai to give her a hand—he had proved quite good at getting her out of it last night, even if she still had to ask one of the other women to put her back into it this morning. Now she'd have to find someone else.

The camera crew that had filmed them this morning had followed Kai out the door, so she was alone when she washed down the counters for a final time, undid her apron, hung it up and entered the main room of the bunkhouse to head out the front door.

Avery was standing near a large wooden desk in one corner that Boone mostly used to organize Base Camp paperwork. She jumped and spun around when she heard Addison approach. "Oh, my goodness, you scared me to death. I didn't think anyone was still here."

She had a single cameraman with her. A young man named Byron. He'd jumped, too. He steadied the camera he was lugging on his shoulder and pointed it at Addison.

"What were you doing?" Addison asked them.

"Just... you know..."

"No, I don't actually." Addison had expected Avery

to say she was looking for a pen, but she looked so guilty, Addison was curious now.

"Can you keep a secret?" Avery approached her.

"Ye—es."

"You know I want to be an actress, right? And that I'm working on a screenplay?"

Addison nodded.

"Well, this is part of that. Byron is helping me put together little skits and film them to put online. I need to showcase what I can do—and what I can write. We thought the bunkhouse was empty, so we were working on one."

"And you needed Boone's desk."

"Exactly. It's for the skit."

That made sense. "Why is it a secret?"

"Because everyone will want to see them if they know we're making movies. I'm not ready for that. I need a little time. Can you keep this a secret? Please?" Avery looked so desperate, Addison felt for her. She was right; everyone was in everyone else's business here at Base Camp. It was hard to get a moment to yourself.

"Of course I can," Addison assured her.

Avery looked relieved. "You're a lifesaver, Addison. Thank you."

"My pleasure." She walked out the door, realizing too late she should have asked Avery to help with her corset. Then she remembered Byron and his camera, and decided to find a more discreet way to get help with her underthings.

"YOU HAVE TO start somewhere," Kai's sister Celia told him when he called her later that morning. "One step at a time, right? If you try, you can make something of the situation, build your career and eventually you'll get to the place where you're calling the shots, don't you think?"

There was that Ledbetter practicality, Kai thought. If he called his mom or dad, they'd say the same thing. When life handed you an opportunity, you took it and made the most of it.

It was sound advice, but it wasn't satisfying.

"I don't see how I can be on one show that's dedicated to sustainability and be on another show that pushes unsustainable products."

"Isn't there any way beef can be raised sustainably? Push that," Celia said.

Kai sighed. There was, but that wasn't the point. The point was he could already tell he would clash with Linkley on every part of the show. Even if he made sure the beef he cooked was organic and sustainable, he'd have no control over the brands pushed during the commercial breaks.

"You can't change the world all at once," Celia said. "It sounds like an amazing opportunity. Just what you said you wanted to do."

"I've got to run. Thanks for listening," Kai said. He got off the phone as frustrated as he'd been when he'd dialed her number.

He needed to talk to someone else. When Addison came to mind, he shook his head. He'd unloaded enough on her last night. He'd never told anyone outside his family about his early days. Not even any of the men he'd served with. Describing those times to Addison made them too real. He'd never treat his own children like that.

Would he and Addison have kids?

The thought had him stuffing his hands in his pockets. They hadn't talked about that. There was still so much to sort out.

He didn't have much time, though. Neither of them had been ready to announce their engagement this morning; it was still too new. But he'd take her to get a ring soon, and they'd share their news. They needed to set a wedding date. They had a deadline to beat, after all.

But they'd beat it, and that was one less problem to solve.

They had plenty of others left over.

He decided to find Angus or Boone—someone who understood the ins and outs of sustainable food and might have ideas about how to salvage his cooking show.

Feed Your Army.

Hell, no.

Was the price of success really turning his back on everything important to him?

IF SHE DIDN'T get this corset fixed, she was going to scream, Addison thought as she made her way down from the manor at a quarter to five. When she'd arrived there earlier, she'd stepped into pure chaos. The women were trying to clean up from one set of guests and prepare for another set who were due the following day. Riley had tripped and spilled a pot of coffee all over the kitchen floor. Addison had helped clean it up and then gone straight from one chore to another all day. She hadn't had a moment to slip away and fix her corset. Now she was late to help Kai with dinner, but for the first time that day she had a minute to spare—and she'd lost her camera crew. Scanning the encampment, she huffed out a frustrated breath. There was no one around to help her—

No, wait—

The sound of a tent fly being unzipped stopped her in her tracks. Someone was here. Was it Samantha?

No. Curtis. Daisy following at his heels.

He'd have to do, Addison decided. The boning of the corset must have rubbed a welt into her skin by this point. Every move she made was torture, and she honestly thought she might cry if someone didn't help loosen it. He wouldn't see anything. These outfits had so many layers she could strip several of them off and still have more clothes on than she would have worn on a normal summer day.

"Curtis, wait. Can you help me?" she called as he headed off toward the building site.

"What's up?" He turned around at her voice.

"Come here." She gestured impatiently, and when he made his way over, she told him, "I need someone to untie me. It's an emergency."

She tugged him inside her tent, zipped the flap back

up, knelt down on her pallet and presented her back to him. Outside, Daisy whined. "Undo my dress," Addison ordered.

"Uh… Addison. Are you sure—"

She was past caring about modestly. Way past. The corset felt like sandpaper rubbing a wound. "Right now, Curtis!"

Daisy yipped again.

Curtis shushed her. "Okay, okay." He must have caught the desperation in Addison's voice, for his fingers worked at the fastenings of the dress and soon enough he had them off. "I'll leave you to it." He already had a hand on the tent's zipper when she turned on him.

"Curtis, I need you!" Addison got herself under control and lowered her voice as Daisy barked a warning outside. Curtis didn't understand how much pain she was in. "It's not my dress. It's my corset. It's rubbing so bad."

The big man hesitated. "Maybe we should find someone else—"

"Curtis, please! And tell Daisy to stop." Daisy was still barking. She was sure to attract someone's attention.

With a sigh, Curtis shushed the dog again and began to work at the corset lacings, but it took forever for him to get them undone. Crouched in the low tent, her knees aching from the cramped position, Addison wanted to tear the whole outfit off and be done with it.

Instead she stayed still until the knots gave way and

he was able to work the laces until she could breathe freely.

"What masochist did you up this morning?" Curtis chuckled now that the job was done.

"Riley. She didn't mean to screw it up, but we were both in a hurry."

"You want to take that off?"

"No." The dress simply wouldn't work without it. She straightened out the undergarment and realized her shift had become bunched up beneath it. No wonder it had been so uncomfortable. She adjusted its folds to a better arrangement. "Do me up again. Just leave me some breathing room this time. A lot of breathing room."

It took even longer for Curtis to do up the corset again loosely. Addison began to grow aware of the position they were in. Daisy was still whining from time to time outside the tent.

"Hurry up before someone else comes."

"Exactly what I was trying to say before." Another minute went by, Addison counting every second. "There. All done. Now, your dress." He helped her pull it on and got that done up, too. "Right as rain." He undid the tent flap, climbed out and Addison followed him. There was no one in sight except Daisy, who danced with joy at Curtis's feet now that he'd reappeared.

"Thank you," Addison said in relief. "That was perfect. You were fast."

"Magic fingers," Curtis said, gesturing with his

hands. "Don't say I'm not talented."

"You're talented, all right."

She headed for the bunkhouse, breathing freely for the first time that day. The place where the corset had rubbed was still uncomfortable, but she was far better off than she'd been before. She reached the bunkhouse nearly a full half hour after she should have been there.

"Kai? Sorry I'm late. What do you want me to do first?"

The kitchen was empty. Addison was about to go looking for Kai when he came in behind her, went straight to the refrigerator and began to pull out food.

"There you are," she said cheerfully. "Should I chop some onions?" Every meal seemed to start with onions.

"Not today."

"Salad stuff?"

Kai grunted. She wasn't sure what that meant.

"Lettuce first?"

"Look," Kai said, dumping the load of vegetables he'd fetched from the refrigerator onto the counter. "Thanks for coming around and helping all the time, but I don't need you tonight. All right? In fact, maybe you should—" He cut off, but Addison could guess what he meant to say. *Maybe you should leave.*

Addison stilled. What had happened? "But—Why—?" Was Kai still upset about that phone call?

"Can't you give me some space?" he growled.

"Of course." Addison rushed from the room.

CHAPTER TEN

WHEN KAI WOKE up to a torrential downpour slapping against the fly of his tent, he knew the day wasn't going to go well. He'd learned there was no sense trying to avoid getting wet on mornings like these. The best way to keep from spending the rest of the day damp was to dress in the bunkhouse. He threw on yesterday's boxer briefs, gathered new ones and the rest of his clothes, shoved his feet in his boots, climbed out of his tent, getting soaked while zipping the flap back up, and dashed to the bunkhouse to find several soggy Base Camp members already there.

Angus catcalled when he caught sight of Kai in his boxers, and Riley flung her hands up to block her eyes, quickly turning her back to him. Kai hotfooted it to the kitchen, peeled off his soaking drawers, dried off with a towel and dressed in the outfit he'd managed to keep reasonably dry on his dash to the building.

He turned to find a crew filming the whole process.

"You'd better not show my bare ass on TV," he snarled.

"We won't. We'll just save it to blackmail you with later. We got more than your ass," Chris said with a grin. He was an older member of the camera crew. A real smart aleck.

"Out. Out!" Kai wasn't in the mood for the crew's banter. He didn't care if they flashed his genitals to the whole world. His life was already shit. Sleeping alone last night had brought home how badly he was going to miss Addison.

But he'd been hurt before and survived.

The crew retreated. "Got enough footage of you cooking to last a lifetime, anyway," Chris said as they disappeared into the main room, where the cacophony of voices told him more people had arrived. No one would get anything other than the most basic outside chores done on a day like this. People were going to be bored, wet—cranky.

He needed to do what he could to stave that off.

Breakfast burritos it was—with the last of their store-bought tortillas. Everyone loved breakfast burritos. Not fancy, not flashy.

Just pure, yummy calories. One final feast. No more of those until the show was over—without flour, he couldn't make them.

"How can I help?"

Addison stood in the doorway, obviously unsure about her welcome.

She should be, Kai thought. He'd heard enough last night to understand she was having a relationship with Curtis. An intimate relationship.

He'd been fooled by Addison. She'd made him think she was the kind of woman who waited until she really knew a man before she got intimate with him. The kind of woman who'd meant it when she'd agreed to marry him. Instead she'd played him with as much callousness as a hustler on the street.

Now he wanted her gone, before she finished the job of destroying him. He'd only known her a short time, but... damn it... he'd—

No, he told himself. He hadn't fallen in love with her. He wasn't that stupid.

But he was. Stupid enough to pick the same kind of woman he always picked—sexy, flighty, devil-may-care gypsies who set you alight while they were with you—

And then walked away from the blaze without a backward look.

She'd said she'd marry him. Then slipped away into a tent with Curtis, leaving Daisy to guard the door. He couldn't believe how wrong he'd been about her.

"Kai? You seen my paperweight?" Boone stuck his head in the door.

"Paperweight? The bullet one?" It had sat on Boone's desk since Kai had gotten to Base Camp—a large caliber World War II bullet encased in resin.

"That's the one."

"No, man. Sorry."

Boone disappeared, and Kai got back to cooking. What the hell else could he do? Addison hesitated in the doorway.

"Kai—where's the food?" Angus boomed from the

main room. A chorus of "yeahs" followed. He was going to have a mutiny on his hands soon. The quicker he fed them, the quicker they could all get on with their business. Then maybe he'd get some peace and quiet to figure out what the hell he was going to do next.

"Kai—"

"Onions," he snapped, cutting Addison off. He didn't want a conversation. Didn't want excuses or pretenses. She made him sick. He turned his attention to slicing rounds of green pepper, deliberately not looking her way.

"I don't understand what's—"

"We don't have time to talk. We've got a crowd of hungry people." He looked up. Spotted a camera. Fuck.

Addison didn't say another word as they prepped the meal, even when Kai thumped the last of the green peppers in front of her and handed her a knife.

While he prepped the rest of the vegetables, Addison assembled plates, forks, knives and condiments and carried them out in batches to a folding table Kai set up to serve the meal.

Each time she stepped from the kitchen to the main room, the onlookers "oohed" in anticipation. The whole group was in an unsettled mood. They were joking, teasing each other—

But there was tension there, too.

He knew they all were worried about the coming winter—whether they could meet Fulsom's demands or whether they would blow it all and lose everything they'd built. Knew they were wondering what the food supply would look like over the coming months. They were at a crisis, and the snow hadn't even begun to fly yet.

When he and Addison finally carted out the rest of the fixings for the breakfast burritos, the other members of Base Camp hurried to get in line. There was a lot of good-natured pushing and shoving, but again, Kai thought he felt a darker undercurrent.

He wanted the meal done and the people scattered to their work before anything happened.

Someone had pulled out the folding chairs they used for meetings, set them up and scattered them around. Soon the chairs were all occupied, and the meal began. The tension dissipated as bellies warmed and clothes dried. Kai chose a chair near the kitchen, although there wasn't anything left to do there. Addison chose a chair at the far end of the room near Riley and Avery.

Halfway through the meal, Kai noticed something else. Curtis kept glancing from him to Addison and back again, Daisy drowsing on the floor by his side. The muscles in Kai's jaw tightened. The man had courted Addison behind his back. Was sleeping with her. And he had the nerve to sit here and eat Kai's food?

As if he read the condemnation on Kai's face, Curtis handed his plate to Clay, stood up and crossed the room. "In the kitchen. Now."

Kai set his plate down on the floor with a thump and stood to meet him face-to-face. If Curtis had something to say, he'd better say it. "Why don't we do this right here?"

"For fuck's sake—get in the kitchen." Curtis pushed past him and led the way.

Kai stalked after him, itching to punch Curtis's daylights out. A camera crew followed but kept their distance.

Smart move.

"What's the deal between you and Addison?" Curtis demanded.

"What's the deal between *you* and Addison?" Kai countered.

Curtis nodded. "Yeah, I thought so. You saw me in her tent."

"I heard you," Kai corrected. "Fucking couldn't keep your hands off her, could you?"

"I was helping her with—"

Kai shoved him. "Helping her with what? Your fucking d—"

Curtis shoved him back. "Maybe I should help her see what a fucking ass you are—"

"Maybe I should help you see if my foot fits up your ass!"

Curtis threw a punch. Kai blocked it, and they locked together, grappling and swiping at each other, crashing around the kitchen until they fell against a cupboard and made the dishes inside rattle. Curtis lunged to trip him, and they both went down hard but quickly resumed the fight, thrashing around on the floor, each trying to land a punch whenever they could.

"What the hell?" Boone burst into the room. Clay and Angus, too. They quickly separated him from

Curtis. Restrained by his friends, Kai fought to reach him again.

"That asshole thinks he can—"

"He was helping me fix my corset because Riley tightened it too hard and I couldn't breathe," Addison cried. "And you were too damn busy sulking about your TV show to listen to me!"

Kai stiffened. Spotted Addison and the other women grouped in the doorway.

"Oh, my God," Riley said to her. "I'm sorry, Addison. Why didn't you tell me?"

"It didn't seem that bad at first." Addison lifted her hands helplessly.

"TV show?" Boone asked. "What TV show?"

"I've had that happen," Avery said. "It gets worse and worse until you can't stand it another minute."

Kai shook Clay and Angus off. "You couldn't get some woman to help you?" he demanded. It was becoming all too clear he was in the wrong, but he was too far gone to acknowledge that now.

"There was no one else around."

"I was there."

She laughed, a hollow sound. "Where? Outside my tent? Watching me? I didn't know that. Obviously." She shook her head at him. "Did you honestly think I would hit on Curtis right after I agreed to marry you?"

"What TV show?" Boone asked again.

Addison's eyes widened when Kai didn't answer, and he thought she'd turn and flee.

The enormity of his mistake flooded Kai.

Hell, he was a fool. She was right; she'd pledged him her heart. Bared her soul to him. Listened to him bare his.

And he'd jumped to conclusions.

"Nothing happened," Curtis told him. "Nothing is ever going to happen. I'll get my bride soon enough. I know what's it like to lose one to another man. You think I'd do that to you?"

Kai closed his eyes. He'd let his fears get the better of him. Let the stress about the food supply and the cooking show mess with his mind.

"What TV show?" Boone demanded.

As the silence stretched out in the kitchen, Kai realized he'd have to make amends. This was all on him.

"I'm… sorry." Swallowing his pride was one of the hardest things he'd ever done. He opened his eyes and faced them. "I shouldn't have jumped to conclusions."

To his surprise, Curtis chuckled. "Fuck it," he said, a grin turning up one side of his mouth. "It would have taken a saint not to jump to *that* conclusion. I'd have done the same thing." He turned to Addison. "I *was* undressing you," he pointed out.

A smile quirked her lips, too, and Kai relaxed a little. He supposed he could see the humor in the situation. "I guess he's right," she said to Kai. "What you thought was understandable given the circumstances, but I'd never betray you like that. I've made you a promise. I'm going to keep it."

Another memory crashed through Kai—a night when he was eight. Wanda Ledbetter had caught him waiting up for her and Eric when they'd left the kids with a sitter to go to a work party.

"Why aren't you sleeping?" she'd asked, tucking him back into his bed.

"Just wanted to make sure you were coming back."

She'd touched his face. "I will always come back," she'd told him. "I've made you a promise, and I'm going to keep it."

Wanda always had. To this day she and Eric—and his siblings, step- and otherwise—were there whenever he needed them. Some people let you down.

But not all of them. Maybe Addison was more like the Ledbetters and less like the women he'd dated previously.

Kai nodded, the only thing he could do. Then reached out, tugged Addison close and crushed her to his chest.

"I love you," he told her fiercely. "I'm sorry."

"I love you, too." She tilted her chin to look up at him, and he captured her mouth with his, hoping his kiss could say everything he didn't know how to put into words. When her arms wrapped around his neck and she kissed him back, he knew he'd been successful.

Whistles and clapping filled the room, and when he pulled back, Kai let out a ragged breath. "All right. Show's over. Keep moving, citizens; nothing to see here." He waved the rest of them out of the room, but Boone didn't budge.

"I'm waiting," he said.

Kai nodded. "It's called *Feed Your Army*," he said

ruefully and explained the whole thing.

"Sounds like a good step forward for your career," Boone said when he was done. "The name sucks, though."

"I know. Should have told you sooner, but I wasn't sure it was going to pan out."

"Got it. I'll get out of your hair. Good luck with the show."

Addison stepped aside and let him pass by.

When he was gone, Kai kissed her again. "Can you forgive me?"

"You were jealous," she pointed out in a teasing voice.

He tightened his arms around her. "Hey."

"I liked it," she said simply and shrieked when he growled again and kissed her noisily on the neck.

"WHAT WAS THAT call earlier about?" Addison figured it had to be part of the reason Kai had overreacted so strongly. Whatever he'd heard had upset him enough to make him lose all sense of proportion.

"It was Linkley. He wants to change some things." Kai made a face. "He wants to change everything. It's pretty bad."

"Uh-oh. What does he have in mind?"

She listened carefully as he described Linkley's vision for the show, leading Kai to the back of the room when people began to file in to scrape their dirty dishes and stack them neatly by the sink.

"That doesn't sound like your vision for the show at

all," she said when Kai was finished.

"Not much."

"What are you going to do?"

"What can I do? He's the producer. He's the one who can get the show on the air. It'll be my first television gig."

"Second one." She indicated the crew filming them. "Don't discount *Base Camp*."

"Still."

She understood what he meant. This was an opportunity to take a step up in his career. It wasn't smart to waste opportunities.

"What if you try working within the framework that Linkley's given you—but add a little of your own flair?" she said slowly.

"What do you mean?"

"Didn't you ever have to use sneaky tactics as a Navy SEAL?"

"Yeah." Kai chuckled. "All the time."

"Do the same thing here. Sort of slide your message in wherever you can. I bet Avery could help with that."

"Avery? How?" Kai leaned against the counter and folded his arms across his chest.

"She's a screenwriter. You could work with her, plan some bits of dialogue that you can throw in as you cook whatever it is they want you to cook. Sneaky ways to get your point across."

"You think Avery can help me do that?"

"I know she can."

THREE DAYS LATER, Kai was ready to concede that Avery was a genius. She'd helped him come up with lots of throwaway dialogue he could toss out in the middle of cooking. Lines that would seem off the cuff to viewers—and producers. Ones that would be difficult to edit out. They practiced timing until he became an expert at tossing them off during the most important parts of whatever recipe he was preparing—moments the director couldn't cut if they were filming an actual episode.

"There will be a subtext to the whole show," Avery said. "You'll be doing one thing and saying something else, hinting that the recipes you're making are fine for the common man, but that someone who really cares about food—and the planet—would modify the meals in a different way. But the best part is, we'll gear that subtext right at the manliest men watching the show."

"I'm cooking with beef today," Kai said in a hearty, cooking-show-host tone, "but in the field with my Navy SEAL buddies, I'd be using bison." He laughed. "Hardly. Somehow the US Navy never requisitions bison."

"You've got the idea, though," Avery said. "Although you're right; you'll have to be a little subtler than that."

Kai thought it just might work.

Over the course of the following week, they got together to work on the plan as often as they could, so when Kai received the paperwork from Linkley, he signed it and sent it back. Meanwhile, he took every opportunity to spend time with Addison. More than once he found her curled up in a chair reading his cooking notebook like it was a novel.

"Why are you so obsessed with that?" he asked. It was kind of a turn-on, if he was honest.

"Because the more I read, the more obsessed with sustainable food I'm getting."

"Really?" Most of the time he thought he was the only one on the planet interested in that.

"Really. Your approach is different from everything else I've read. Usually, people's suggestions are so basic. Eat plants. Buy local. Your take is more 3-D. You consider everything at once."

Heady praise, Kai thought. Especially coming from someone whose opinion he valued. He wished Linkley felt the same way about the topic.

"I've got to go work with Avery," he told her. "Want to come? I don't get to spend enough time with you these days."

"We spend every night together," she pointed out. "And every breakfast, lunch and dinner."

"That's not nearly enough." Kai pulled her close, kissed her hard and stifled a groan. "I want you right now."

"Later," Addison promised. "I'm supposed to meet Samantha. She's showing me around the gardens again. I feel like I want to know the whole process from start to finish. From garden to plate."

"I like it when you talk dirty to me."

They were both late to their meetings by the time they pulled apart, and Kai had to admit Addison's interest in the topics he loved most fired him up. He couldn't wait until they cleaned up from dinner and had the rest of the night together.

Only when Linkley's secretary rang him back the next day did Kai recognize the next hiccup in their plan. When he hung up, he searched out Curtis and told him what had happened. Their friendship had settled back to a solid place, and Kai was embarrassed he'd ever suspected Curtis of wrongdoing.

"They want to film the pilot episode on Halloween? Don't they realize that's a national holiday?" Curtis teased.

"Apparently not," Kai answered his grin with one of his own. "I already told Addison I'd help her set up for the gala. She's pretty nervous about it. I don't want to ditch her."

"I'm sure she'd understand."

He was pretty sure she would, too. Addison was as accommodating as ever these days, and even if they only got to see each other at rare moments outside of cooking, they made the most of those. He was beginning to get used to having her around—and beginning to depend on her, if he was honest with himself. Her constant presence in the kitchen with him smoothed out his days and gave him more time to work with the others in between times. They'd done what they could to shore up the food supply, planting as many potatoes as they could in the greenhouses and trying to save the wheat, but they'd had to admit that experiment was a failure.

Kai was afraid it was going to be an uncomfortable winter. He was used to hardship, and he was sure he and the other men could get by on meat and vegetables, but hungry people were cranky people, and people who weren't getting the kind of food they liked were even crankier. He needed a plan, which meant spending every extra moment in the garden and greenhouses with the others, estimating what they could grow in the coming months.

When he slipped into the tent that night, found Addison there ahead of him and told her his news, she only said, "It'll be fine; I'll have a ton of help. You just come wearing that toga. That'll be good enough for me."

"What toga?" he asked distractedly. They'd long ago brought her sleeping gear into his tent and zipped their sleeping bags together on top of their sleeping pads. Snuggled in the warm nest they'd created for themselves, he was far too busy exploring her body to listen too hard to her words.

"The one I left here in the tent the other day."

Kai broke away from her and looked around but didn't see it, but it was dark and the cramped quarters were full of his belongings. "Must have pushed it to the side and not even noticed. I'll find it in the morning." He got back to touching Addison.

"Sounds good. We can do a test run. Oh, Kai—"

Kai was too busy rolling her on top of him, lifting her shoulders and taking one of her nipples into his mouth to answer.

CHAPTER ELEVEN

HALLOWEEN DAWNED COOL and crisp, with a crystal-clear blue sky that promised a fine day and an even colder night.

Mid-morning, Kai passed the rest of the men split into groups working hard to frame in and roof the rest of the tiny houses they'd need for married couples before spring made it possible to build again.

One of those would be his soon, and he felt a pang of remorse that he wasn't helping, but Linkley and his crew would arrive soon to film the pilot episode of *Feed Your Army*, and Kai needed to be ready for them.

As he walked, he practiced all the throwaway quips he and Avery had written and she'd made him rehearse over and over until they fell off his tongue like he'd made them up on the spot. He hoped their idea would work, and he could subversively take over the show and make it what he wanted it to be.

There was still the chance he could blow this whole thing and be right back where he started. But he wasn't going to anticipate trouble. There was trouble enough in the world without making up more, as his mom always said.

"There's the man of the hour," Linkley boomed when he arrived in a limousine an hour later. Short, cocky, suited up for a New York boardroom rather than a fall Montana morning, he made quick work of the introductions and paced straight into the bunkhouse to get the lay of the land. "Christ, would you look at this place? All right, everyone; get to work. It ain't going to be easy to film here. We should have brought you in to do this on set, but Renata wouldn't agree to it. Between you and me, kid, that woman's a ball-buster."

Kai had to bite back a smile. He and everyone else at Base Camp already knew that.

It took more than an hour for Linkley's crew to set up, creating an island countertop in the middle of the small kitchen for Kai to work at, setting up bright lights and reflectors. Meanwhile, Linkley introduced him to Mike Machamp, the show's director, an unassuming man with a voice as loud as Linkley's when he needed it to be.

"Think tractors, VFW halls, pancake breakfasts and Fourth of July parades," Machamp said. "Middle America. Salt of the earth. Men who really like a steak. That's your audience."

"Hell, yeah." Kai boomed back at him. He and Avery had decided he'd play this the way Linkley wanted—except for the parts where he wouldn't. If they wanted a man's man, that's exactly what they'd get.

"Right. Exactly." Machamp brightened at his response. "Except you can't swear. This is a family-friendly show."

"Gotcha." Kai felt as cocky as Linkley. He was ready for this. He'd get his message out, with or without their approval.

"All right. Let's get some makeup on this soldier," Linkley ordered.

"Sailor," Kai corrected, then waved away Linkley's questioning look. "Not important."

Ages passed until they were ready to actually film, but finally everything was in place. The director counted him in, Kai looked into the camera and began to speak.

"Hello, I'm Kai Green, and I'll be your host for *Feed Your Army*. After spending over a decade protecting this great country as a Navy SEAL, I know all about working up a real appetite, and I'm here today to help you feed your army at home, no matter how big—or hungry—it may be." There. At least he'd set the record straight about the branch he'd served in.

Linkley was grinning and nodding. Machamp seemed pleased, too. Kai reached down beneath the counter to where the crew had placed all the props he needed and brought out a cutting board and a slab of steak. "We're going to make chili today. Real manly chili, not some watered-down version your wife makes to feed to her sewing circle. Something that will satisfy the hunger you have for meat."

As Kai continued reading from the teleprompter, he decided it was time to add a comment or two of his own. He worked on cutting the steak into chunks.

"I'm working with beef today, because beef is standard issue in most grocery stores. But one of the best things about being a man is you get to make up your own mind. That means you can substitute your own ingredients. Want to go for a real manly meal? Try some Grade A bison meat in your chili. Montana raised and grown—mm, mmm that's good stuff."

Machamp frowned, and Linkley's brows met in the middle, but Kai charged on, going back to reading straight from the teleprompter, and they let it pass, just like Avery had said they would. He saved his message about bean to meat ratio for when he was frying up the meat.

"Now, I know some people say a real chili has no beans. I know others who say the beans make the chili. What I say is, we're all hungry, we're all on a budget and, heck, we all want to do our part to halt the damage CO_2 emissions can cause. So cut your chili with beans. They're tasty, satisfying, light on the wallet—and light on the planet, too. If you're a real renegade, like me, you might even throw in lentils." He kept busy the whole time and immediately switched back to the teleprompter's words. Once again, the producer's and director's worried expressions slipped back into approval. He'd made sure that while he was speaking, he grabbed the pan and flipped the frying meat like he would pancakes with a jerk of his wrist, a cool move it wouldn't be easy for them to cut out. He caught Byron and another of Renata's crew members exchanging a look as they filmed the *Feed Your Army* crew filming him. He'd better make sure he didn't overdo things.

But by the time filming was over, he'd managed to slip all but one comment into the show's narrative. He was riding high on his effort, proud of his cooking and his ability to get his message across.

"Good stuff," Linkley said. "A little too much off the cuff, but we'll polish that out of you."

Like hell, Kai thought.

It seemed to take just as long for Linkley's crew to pack up again, but finally the limo and trucks pulled out of Base Camp and it was time to get ready for the masquerade ball. Back when they'd gone to Alice's for a fitting, he'd been pleased with the way she'd managed to put his Roman senator's costume together so he wouldn't be losing his sheet all night or mistakenly baring his butt during a dance number or some other inauspicious time. He realized now he'd forgotten to look for it in his tent, and he went to find it. He was looking forward to going to the manor and telling Addison all about filming the pilot.

When he arrived at his tent, however, he couldn't find the toga anywhere. Kai scrambled around, finally pulling everything out of his tent and putting it back piece by piece.

Shit. If he was late, he'd disappoint Addison on her big night, and he didn't want to do that.

Kai strode back to the bunkhouse, noting the camp had cleared out. They'd agreed they'd take turns on guard duty tonight during the party, each of them spending an hour on patrol. Walker and Clay were taking the first shift. He'd have his turn late tonight. He could see people on their way to the manor. Only Boone was around when he burst inside. Dressed as a pirate, he looked suitably swashbuckling.

"I can't find my toga," Kai told him.

"Seriously?"

"Seriously. I wanted to be at the manor an hour ago. I need a costume, Boone."

Boone thought fast. "Curtis has two Dracula costumes. Alice sent him two versions to try."

"I don't want to copy him." He was supposed to match Addison's Cleopatra costume.

"Buddy, there's bound to be a half dozen Draculas at any Halloween party. He won't care."

Kai felt funny about looking in another man's tent, but he was desperate, and Boone was with him to vouch that he hadn't gone through anything private. The costume was tossed right on his bedroll, anyway, so it was no big deal to reach in and pull it out.

"See you up at the manor," Boone said. "Hope it fits."

"Me, too." Curtis was brawnier than he was, so at least he didn't have to worry about the costume being too tight. As it was, he had to loop a belt around the pants Alice had provided to keep them from sliding down around his ankles. The shirt and pants were basic but dressy. A black sash covered his belt. It was the cape that made the costume, and this one was an ankle-length black satin number lined with scarlet. The mask covered the top half of his face, with holes for his eyes. Satisfied that at least he wasn't wearing street clothes to the ball, he half jogged up the path to the manor. The last thing he wanted to do was miss Addison's special night.

"HOW DID KAI lose his costume?" Riley asked several hours later. Like Addison, she was contemplating several Draculas converged in one corner of the ball-room having a toast.

The Russells had provided a huge buffet for the ball and an equally generous bar, which their guests seemed determined to drink dry. Addison had drunk several glasses of wine herself, and the ballroom had a soft glow that made everything seem beautiful.

She'd done it—pulled off a ball she could be proud of, and everyone at Base Camp was enjoying them-selves, along with their guests. She'd met many people from town and was pleased to find that all of them treated her like she belonged here at Westfield.

It was like she'd finally come—

Home.

"I have no idea," she said hurriedly, not ready to test that thought. "But then, he is a man…"

"You said a mouthful."

"Are you having fun?" Alice Reed asked, handing Addison a new glass of wine as she joined them. She was dressed like a fairy godmother. Addison thought the costume suited her.

"I've been too nervous to have fun," Addison told her. "But I think it's going well."

"I had a hunch you needed the chance to shine,"

Alice said. "Isn't she great at throwing events?" she asked Riley.

"She's terrific! She'd better watch out, or we'll make her do all the work at the B and B."

"Good idea." Alice winked at Addison and slipped away before Addison could say anything. Boone came to find Riley, and Addison looked around for Kai. It was warm in the ballroom despite the cool temperatures outside. Music swelled again, and a murmur rose as people found partners and began to dance. Addison decided to sit this one out. There was supposed to be a Regency number coming up—they'd coached the musicians to intersperse them between the waltzes and other dance numbers. She couldn't wait to participate. Kai was a wonderful dancer, and she'd gotten the hang of it after a lot of practice.

A woman in a mermaid costume caught her eye. She'd arrived recently, and Addison couldn't place her. She was statuesque, and her costume was to die for, all strategically placed sequins that left little to the imagination, with a mask that covered all but her eyes. She wondered who in Chance Creek could afford a costume like that. Whoever it was certainly liked the free bar. Addison had seen her go back for refills on some kind of colorful mixed drink several times already. As she watched, the stranger threw her head back and laughed at something her current partner said, but Addison didn't think she'd come with anyone—or at least she danced with a new man every song.

"Your ball is a huge success," Maud called as she

212 | CORA SETON

danced by with James. Those two seemed to be having a wonderful time together. So was everyone, Addison thought happily. She'd come into her own putting on this party.

"You are hereby in charge of all the balls at Westfield," Riley said, echoing her thoughts. "I can't believe you did this all yourself."

"I know," Avery said, joining them. "It's amazing!"

"I had a lot of help," Addison said. The ball wouldn't have been half so wonderful without the aid of the Russells—and the props Felicity had sent.

A cheer came from the Draculas in the corner as they toasted one another and downed another drink.

"But I'm a little worried everyone's getting wasted," she added.

"Everyone who isn't pregnant," Savannah said glumly. She was sipping a virgin margarita, beautiful in a witch costume despite her growing belly.

"I think it's good for people to let off a little steam once in a while," Avery put in. "Everyone's so uptight all the time."

"I'm not uptight," Addison said, stung, even though Avery wasn't addressing her specifically, then she had to laugh at herself. Thank goodness Kevin had thought she was. What if she'd stayed with him? She'd never have met Kai. "In fact, I think I'm three sheets to the wind." She tried to put her glass of wine down on the nearest table but missed the first time. "Whoops."

Savannah took the glass and set it firmly on the table. "You need some coffee."

"I need Kai," Addison corrected her. She wanted to kiss the man she loved. The man who loved her.

Right now.

BOONE WAS RIGHT; there were Draculas everywhere, Kai thought as he went to fetch another round of drinks for the Vlad Patrol, as a bunch of them had named themselves. Boone had also been right that Curtis didn't care in the least that he'd taken his spare costume.

"The more the merrier," he'd said in his best Dracula imitation, which wasn't very good. But no one had minded; the drinks were flowing freely. Probably too freely.

Still, they'd all been so worried these past few weeks, everyone needed to relax for a night. Tomorrow they'd get back to work—and worrying. He had decided to enjoy himself while he could.

"Here you go," the bartender said, passing Kai a tray filled with drinks.

Kai balanced it carefully and waved at another Dracula who'd just come in the door. "Come on, Vlad. Over here. Join the fun."

The man followed him willingly.

"I'm Kai Green. Who are you? I can't tell a damn thing with everyone wearing masks."

"Evan Delaney. I'm from out of town, but I couldn't pass this up."

"Of course not; it's the party of the century." The floor was clogged with dancers, and it wasn't easy to pass through them and keep the tray balanced. Trust him to upend it and make a mess. He didn't want to ruin Addison's evening, so he kept a tight grip on it. "Who are you here with?"

"My wife. She's around here somewhere. She's a mermaid. I had to hang back and take a call out in the car."

"Lucky guy." He'd seen the mermaid. She had one hell of a body and wasn't afraid to show it. If Kai was this man, he'd stick closer to her. He had a feeling she already had half a dozen phone numbers tucked into that tight-fitting costume.

"Who's that Cleopatra?" the man asked, craning his head to get a better look.

Kai swung around to look.

"That's my fiancée," he said. Someone bumped him, and both he and Evan grabbed for the tray of drinks.

"That was a close one."

"No shit." Kai turned to angle through the crowd, anxious to reach the waiting knot of Draculas. He noticed Addison was edging in the same direction, probably looking for him. He tried to raise a hand to get her attention, but the tray tipped, and he grabbed it again.

Evan kept his gaze on Addison, until Kai wondered if he'd have to speak to him about it. Addison caught sight of him and Evan, and made a beeline for them.

"Look at all these Draculas! Damn good thing I can tell my baby anywhere," she called out as she headed their way. She'd been drinking, too, Kai noted fondly. They'd have a party of their own later by themselves in their tent.

"Addi—" His words died in his throat when Addison ran straight up to Evan, seized his face in her hands and planted a kiss on his lips.

SHE WAS KISSING someone, but it wasn't Kai.

Addison realized her mistake almost as soon as her lips touched the man's mouth. She put her hands flat on the stranger's chest and shoved—hard—nearly stumbling back against a pair of dancers.

Crap, crap, crap. Who had she kissed?

"Sorry. Sorry!" she called to the Dracula. "My bad. Where's my man?" Heck, she was drunk, wasn't she? She hadn't had this much alcohol in years. Usually, she kept a cool head while her guests celebrated. She got high off throwing a good party—not from imbibing the alcohol she served.

The room spun, and she tried to stay upright.

The Dracula with the drink tray ripped his mask off. "Addison, what the hell?"

"I thought he was you!" This was awful. Kai was pissed—and hurt by the looks of it.

"Addison?" The other Dracula pulled of his mask.

"Evan? What are you doing here?"

"Felicity demanded that we come. She wanted to surprise you."

Addison laughed then sobered when she took in Kai's expression. "This is my brother-in-law," she explained over the noise of the music, then turned back to Evan. "Consider me surprised. I'm so embarrassed.

Where's Felicity?"

"I haven't found her yet. She's dressed in a mermaid costume," Evan said.

Oh, hell. Suddenly she was stone-cold sober. That mermaid was three sheets to the wind—dancing with every man who asked.

What was wrong with her sister?

"She's over there—" Addison didn't even get to finish her sentence before a shrill voice she recognized pierced through the din.

"Whoo-hooo!" Felicity started making her way toward them. "Kai Green, you are just as sexy in person as you are on-screen."

Kai sent Addison a searching look. Addison grabbed his hand and tugged him close. The drinks on his tray sloshed dangerously. "We've got to stop this. She's drunk. And we're being filmed."

"In fact, everyone is sexy. This is a sexy, sexy group," Felicity drawled.

"Felicity, you're making a scene, honey," Evan took her arm and tried to steer her away. Felicity refused to budge.

"I'm not making a scene. There was already a scene." She circled her finger, taking in him, Kai and Addison. "And there are Draculas everywhere. Why the hell are there so many Draculas?"

She swayed a little. Evan propped her up. "Honey, seriously. Time to go." He shot an apologetic look at Kai. "Cannot hold her liquor," he said with the patience of a long-suffering man.

"My sister—this is all my sister's doing. This fantastic party," Felicity said. "But she wouldn't be here if not for me. I'm the one who got her to say yes!"

"Evan, get her out of here," Addison urged him. Who knew what Felicity was going to say next. "Why aren't you in Rome?"

"It's been pretty rough since you left," Evan told her. "Come on, Felicity," he added.

"Felicity, it's time for you to go," Addison told her sister.

"Don't act like you're not coming, too," Felicity crooned at her. "Sister mine, it's October thirty-first. The game is over. You won. You can start saying no again. Let's go home."

Addison swallowed hard, hoping no one had heard her, but when she glanced at Kai, she knew immediately he had.

"Game?" Kai asked. "What's she talking about? What game? What does she mean she got you to say yes?"

"We made a bet." Felicity shrieked as Evan picked her up and threw her over his shoulder. The rest of her drink splashed to the floor. "She had to say yes to everything for a month. And she did it. She even said yes to you, you silly man! Silly SEAL. Silly, silly SEAL." She dropped her glass and slapped Evan's butt with both hands like it was a pair of bongo drums.

Addison cringed. She'd never seen Felicity so out of control before, and she prayed she could convince Kai not to listen to anything she'd said.

But then Felicity lifted her head again. "You won, sis. You stuck with it and you won. My life is yours, and I get to go to fucking Rome." She fished around in the bosom of her gown and tossed a something that landed at Addison's feet. Addison bent and scooped it up automatically. "My keys," Felicity called back as Evan hauled her away. "The penthouse is all yours. Enjoy!"

CHAPTER TWELVE

"WHAT THE HELL was that?" Kai demanded.

Addison just shook her head, as if she couldn't find the words to speak. All around them, guests stood in clusters, watching them, whispering about them, pointing at Felicity being hauled out of the room.

"That was your sister?"

"Yes," she finally said. "I don't know what got into her. Something's wrong. She isn't usually like that."

"Hell, yeah, something's wrong." He snatched the keys out of her hand. "What are these for? Why did she say her penthouse is yours now?"

"Because—we—I—" Addison lifted her hands helplessly.

Kai had had enough. He didn't know what was going on, and he needed to find out now. "Hey, you! Put down that mermaid!" He strode after Evan, who was still fighting his way toward the door, Felicity still slung over his shoulder. "You two don't get to leave until I know what's going on here." Addison ran to keep up with them.

"Look, my wife is drunk. She's upset." Evan half turned.

"Felicity, take back your keys," Addison said desperately.

"I'm not drunk, and I'm not taking them back," Felicity hollered over Evan's shoulder, her skimpy costume on the verge of becoming all too revealing. "If I've got to go to Rome, you have to live in my penthouse. That's the deal." She arched around farther to get a look at Kai, and pointed to Addison. "You think this girl came here because she likes sleeping in tents? You think she's going to marry the kind of man who cooks for a living? She doesn't want to live with a bunch of cows. Oh, excuse me—bison." Felicity over-enunciated the word. "She wants a penthouse. My penthouse. Money to spend. Fancy parties. A rich husband, too! And she'll do what it takes to get it—including saying yes to every single thing for a month." She pointed at Kai. "Including saying yes to you!"

"Jesus, Felicity." Evan set her down hard on the floor. Felicity wavered, and he propped her up with an arm around her waist. "I'm sorry," he said to Addison. "I knew this was a horrible idea. She's freaking out about the move. Your mom's being awful."

Addison nodded, but her face was white as a sheet.

Kai could barely hear what they were saying. His ears were buzzing. He felt like everyone else in the room was suddenly very far away.

Including saying yes to you.

What had Felicity meant? Was she saying Addison had lied? That she didn't really mean it when she'd agreed to marry him?

"Why?" he demanded suddenly, ignoring the conversations spinning around him. The others turned to him, but none of them answered, so he repeated his question. "Why? Why did you have to say yes for a month?"

Addison's gaze turned pleading, but he waited her out. Something was wrong here. Very wrong. He had the feeling the next few minutes would turn his life on its head.

"Because of the book," Felicity said with a laugh. *"The Freedom of Yes."*

Kai dimly remembered the title. It had been a splash with the self-help circuit some months back. Its cover everywhere you looked. But what did that have to do with—

"We made a deal," Felicity went on, gesturing wildly. "If she said yes to everything for one month, she could have my penthouse. And she did. No matter what I threw at her, she kept agreeing. Hope you're happy," she said to Addison and began to cry.

"Felicity." Addison reached for her sister, turning a look on Kai like he was the one who'd done something wrong.

"So—this was all a lie? Every part of it?" If she had to say yes to everything, did that include—? Kai sucked in a breath. "You mean I forced you to have sex with me?"

"No!" Addison's cheeks went crimson. "Of course not, Kai!"

"Then what? What were the rules to your little game?"

"I... had to say yes to anything that wouldn't hurt me. But, Kai—"

"Including marrying me? None of that was real?"

"It was real—"

Kai had heard enough. He tossed Addison the keys. She missed, and they skidded across the floor, but he didn't care. He turned to find Boone approaching them.

"I hope like hell you've got a backup bride lined up," he snarled at his friend then turned and stormed out.

ADDISON WATCHED THE crowd part around Kai as he strode out of the room. She wanted to yell after him—to chase him down—but she knew the only thing was to let him cool down and talk to him when they were all sober. The night was a disaster.

"Hey, let's stay and enjoy the party," she heard Felicity slur, but she knew without turning that Evan was finally, blessedly, hauling her away.

Someone pressed a handkerchief into her hand.

Maud.

"Thank you." Addison hadn't even felt the tears streaming down her face.

"This is a bad business, but it'll work out, you'll see." Maud sounded too worried to convince Addison she believed that. "Don't you worry about a thing, pet.

The sun will come up tomorrow, and all will be well again."

"I don't think so." Addison wiped her eyes. She knew she should go after Felicity and find out what had happened to set off such a breakdown. Or go after Kai and try to explain everything that had transpired. But first she needed to catch her breath.

How had everything gone so off course?

The music started up again, and slowly couples returned to dancing. Several cameramen remained focused on her, but others drifted off to film the action elsewhere.

"See?" Maud said. "Life goes on. It always does, no matter what the trouble."

"Kai hates me now," Addison said. She could only imagine what he thought. Her sister had presented everything in the worst light.

"Rather the opposite, I'd say. He loves you. That makes it harder. But he'll see the truth in time. You might have come for reasons other than love, but love found you, didn't it?"

"It did," Addison admitted. "I love him so much. I don't want to leave." She realized it was true. "This life is so much better than the one I was trying to have."

"Of course, dear."

"Addison."

She turned in surprise to find Evan had returned.

"Where's Felicity?"

"Sleeping in the limo. I'd say she's down for the count. Listen, I'm sorry—I knew this wouldn't be a good idea, but she insisted on coming."

"I thought you'd already gone to Europe."

"We pushed our travel back until tomorrow so we could attend. I thought it was because she wanted to see the decorations she'd sent—and to say goodbye again, of course. I should have known there was more going on that that."

"She's afraid," Addison told him.

"I know. I didn't expect it. She's traveled so much before."

"But never more than a few days without Mom. She's scared Mom's right; that she can't do it on her own."

"She won't be on her own. She has me," Evan said.

"You're so good for my sister," Addison said truthfully.

"I know I am. But she's good for me, too, ninety-nine percent of the time. Don't hold this against her for too long. She's going to miss you, you know. She's scared of leaving you, too."

Addison nodded, so grateful Evan was in her sister's life. "Just keep her away from the booze," she implored him.

"Will do," he said. "Look, about the penthouse. It's yours. The paperwork is signed and ready to go. You'll find it on the kitchen table. I hope you enjoy it as much as we have." He handed her the keys he must have picked up off the floor. "Try to hold on to these." He smiled, and Addison's heart squeezed. "Really—enjoy."

Addison didn't know what to say. The keys were

cool and heavy in her hand. Once she'd thought they represented the future she wanted. Now…

"My dear, where is your heart?" Maud intruded, seeming to grasp the situation without much of an explanation. "Here or New York?"

"Here," Addison said without hesitation. "It's here. With Kai."

"Listen to it. It'll never steer you wrong."

Addison opened her fingers. Stared at the key ring, then held it out to Evan. "I don't need it."

Evan nodded as if not surprised. "I've been watching the show," he explained. "Anyone can see you love it here. And love Kai. But are you sure? I'm going to list it if you don't take it. We don't intend to move back anytime soon."

She hesitated, her fingers still around the keys that were resting in Evan's palm. If he sold it, that meant no backup plan. She'd be going all-in here at Base Camp. If Kai didn't change his mind—

She'd be right back where she started from.

But that was okay, she told herself. She'd learned so much about herself in the past few weeks. She was strong. Capable. She could write her own future if this path was a dead end.

She had to fight for Kai—for her life here.

She let go of the keys, and Evan took them.

"Good luck," she told him. "I hope you two are very happy in Rome."

"I hope you come and visit us really soon. Your sister misses you already."

"I miss her, too."

He backed up a step. "You're sure?" He raised the hand that held the keys. "You want me to list it?"

Addison was as sure as she'd ever been in her life. "Yes."

"SOME NIGHT, HUH?" Avery said the next morning.

Kai grunted. She was the first person he'd seen since he'd gotten up at the same time he'd always done, did his yoga routine, meditated—rather unsuccessfully—and gone for a run. He'd slept alone last night. He didn't know where Addison had slept—probably on a flight to New York, back to her sister's penthouse. Her prize for fooling him.

He was prepping breakfast, as usual, but he wondered if he was wasting his time. The whole camp seemed to have decided to sleep in after their late night.

As for Addison—he didn't even want to think about her. Everything she'd done was fake. Everything she'd said.

She'd never been serious about him at all.

He kept running back over their time together in his mind, trying to figure out what parts were real and when she'd been acting. It must have all been an act, he finally concluded, because he couldn't find a way to distinguish one set of her behaviors from another.

"Breakfast will be in about a half hour," he said shortly.

"I didn't come for food. I came to talk."

"Not much in the mood."

"I can see that." But Avery didn't leave. Instead, she popped up onto the counter, legs swinging.

Kai turned and glared at her.

She didn't budge.

"Say what you have to say."

"I think you're making a mistake. Addison might have come here on a dare or something, but she fell in love with you."

Kai grunted again. He didn't think so.

"You need to—"

Kai's phone buzzed in his pocket, and he pulled it out. "Kai here," he said when he'd answered it.

"Kai! It's Linkley. Want to have a little chat about your pilot."

"Uh… sure." This wasn't what he needed, but he didn't have a fiancée anymore. He didn't want to lose his cooking show, too.

"The studio was really pleased with what they saw. They want to run with the show. Ten episodes for the first season."

"That's… great." It didn't feel great, though. He wondered if anything ever would again. "Really—that's great," he said again, trying to sound more enthusiastic.

"Just one thing," Linkley went on.

Kai gripped the phone so hard he thought it might shatter. One thing? He didn't think he could take one more thing. Not when the woman he'd thought he loved had turned out to be a liar and fraud. "What's that?"

"This… subtext you're trying to push. It's got to go.

You read the teleprompter and you stick with the program. You're not a comedian."

"I wasn't trying to be," Kai said slowly.

"Improv's not your best skill," Linkley said. "But you look good. The studio really likes the way you look."

Kai tried for a reply. Couldn't come up with one. He *looked* good? What the hell did that mean? He was trying to change the world; who cared how he looked while he was doing it?

"The business is the business, kid. You understand? Don't try to outsmart it. Roll with it. Do what you're told. Can you do that?"

"I... I'm excited to work with you, sir."

"We'll send the paperwork." Linkley hung up before he could reply.

"Who was that?" Avery asked when he pocketed his phone.

"I got my cooking show. Ten episodes." Kai turned back to the meal he was preparing, and for the first time in his life, he didn't feel like cooking. He braced his hands on the counter and bowed his head.

Fuck. First Addison, now this.

Avery jumped down and came to stand next to him. "Tell me."

"It's not going to be my show at all. They're going to kill my brand before I even get started. I'm going to end up a spokesman for all the things I don't believe in."

"Then don't do it."

"I may not get another chance!"

Avery surveyed him. "Go ask Addison. See what she suggests."

"Addison's gone." The sentence stuck in his throat, and Kai swallowed hard.

"She's in her tent," Avery contradicted. "Sleeping off her hangover like everyone else. Boone found her another sleeping bag. Seems you had hers." She smiled. "Talk to her. No, better yet—listen to her. Hear her side of the story. You might learn something."

"Addison's in her tent?" But why? She'd gotten the keys to the penthouse she so desperately wanted.

"Because she loves you," Avery said simply.

"No, she doesn't."

"Yes, she does. Maybe this all started with some stupid deal she made with her sister, but then it turned into something else. I've seen the way she looks at you, Kai. She's not faking that. Give her a chance."

For one long moment, he almost agreed, but then he remembered everything Felicity said. Remembered the way Addison had thought the show was fake.

She hadn't come here to marry him.

It was time to move on.

WHEN ADDISON WOKE up, she had one blessed second before all the events of the previous evening crashed into her consciousness. She groaned and pulled the sleeping bag over her head. She wasn't sure why she'd thought she could fix things if she stayed. She'd slinked out of the ball, Avery and Maud assuring her they'd take care of everything, and after making a half-hearted attempt to find Kai had simply gone to bed.

"Addison?" a female voice said outside.

"Mmm?" she managed.

"Come on. Let's go to the manor." It was Riley.

Addison wanted to ignore her, but she had a feeling Riley wouldn't stand for being ignored. Against her better judgement, she climbed out of the sleeping bag, gathered some clothes and opened the tent flap.

It was a long trudge up the hill. Thankfully, Riley didn't seem to need to talk. At the manor, Riley ushered her upstairs.

"Take a good, long, hot shower," she said. "You'll feel better. I'll help you dress. Then you can go find Kai."

Addison hesitated by the bathroom door. "Maybe I should just leave."

"Honey, you're not responsible for how your sister behaves," Riley pointed out. "We don't want you to leave."

"But Felicity was right," Addison felt compelled to say. "I did come here because I wanted her stupid penthouse."

"And then you fell in love with Kai, right? And everything else about Base Camp. You had a blast putting on the ball, didn't you?"

"Yes." Addison wondered if she'd ever be able to say that word again without thinking of her time at Base Camp.

"Then that's that."

"You think it's really so simple?" Addison leaned against the doorframe. "I'm not sure Kai will see it that way."

"You won't know unless you ask him."

"But—"

"He loves you, too," Riley insisted. "Now, take your shower, we'll get you dressed and we'll go find him. Together."

Addison did so, and when she was ready, she and Riley walked down to Base Camp in silence, Addison fighting off tears. She'd gotten to know every step of the path between the camp and the manor. She loved this walk. Loved all of it.

Loved Kai.

Was she about to lose everything?

"There he is now. Looking for you, I'd say." Riley pointed to Kai exiting the bunkhouse. Addison swallowed hard as Kai spotted them and stopped. He waited for them to reach him, and Addison's gut tightened as they approached. Would he yell? Swear? Tell her to pack her things and go?

Several cameramen grouped around them, and she wished to God they could have this conversation alone, but maybe this was a type of humility, baring your mistakes in front of the world. Maybe other people could learn from the mess she'd made of things.

Kai bowed his head, and when he looked up she read resignation in his eyes. "Would you walk with me?" he asked.

"Yes." Addison bit her lip when he winced. Every

yes now seemed fake, no matter how heartfelt it was, and it must sound fake to him, too. He was pissed. He was going to ask her to leave. She couldn't imagine what her life was going to look like without this place—

Without Kai.

They turned toward the track that led down to Pittance Creek. Addison wasn't sure whether to break right into an explanation, or wait—

"Avery says I should talk to you," Kai said stiffly.

Addison nearly quailed at how distant he sounded but forced herself to speak up. "I want to apologize for what happened last night."

"Can you explain what's really going on? I'll try to listen."

He was making an effort to hold back his anger—and pain, Addison thought. It hurt so bad to know she'd hurt him, especially when she knew the ways he'd been hurt before. Why had she been so careless with the love of a man like this? She deserved everything she got, but first she was going to fight to change his mind.

"Just like Felicity said, it all started with a book. *The Freedom of Yes.*"

"I've heard of it."

"Well, I was reading it. And Felicity saw it and started teasing me. She's always saying I'm too uptight. That I plan too much. Worry too much. While she just goes and gets what she wants. It was the same weekend she told me she and Evan were moving to Rome. I guess… I guess she was trying to distract me from that. Distract both of us. She was afraid of leaving—I didn't realize that then." Tears stung her eyes. "I should have been paying more attention."

"So, you were reading a book." He wasn't going to let her off easy. Addison took a breath and went on.

"She kept at me. Dangled her penthouse in front of me, said I could have it—if I said yes for one month. She was leaving, and I was going to be stuck in Connecticut, living a life I didn't like—"

"And you agreed to that."

"I agreed to that." She wished she could say otherwise. Shame flared through her at the mess she'd made.

"Whose idea was it to apply to marry me? Felicity's?"

Addison nodded.

"Did she… did she make you dress like you did in the audition tape?"

Heat suffused Addison's face. "Yeah, she did. She bought me the clothes I wore here, had my hair and makeup done. She controlled all of it."

Kai seemed to consider this. "How do you normally dress?"

"Well, I'm an insurance actuary, so I—" She broke off when Kai tilted his head back and guffawed. "What?"

"Oh, man. The Universe is fucking with me. Big time!" He continued walking, shaking his head, and after a moment Addison caught up. "The whole idea of my ad was that for once I was going to pick a sensible woman. A safe one. A practical one. I guess that's what I got."

"Who do you usually date?" Addison wasn't sure what to make of that. She was sensible, but she didn't know about... safe. That sounded so boring.

"Women who knit caps for surfers. Which, let me guess: you don't actually do."

"Nope." She waited a beat. "So, I'm not the kind of woman you even like."

Kai was silent a minute. "That's not true. I liked you a lot, right from the start. Even though you weren't knitting."

"I liked you a lot, too."

He stopped, and Addison waited. "Maybe fate knew what it was doing after all," he said quietly.

"Maybe. Kai, I'm sorry for all of it. I never meant to hurt you. Felicity and I really did think the show was staged, and the moment I arrived none of that mattered anyway. I fell for you fast."

Kai stilled. "Did you?"

She felt heat rise in her cheeks. "Actually, I fell for you a long time before that. I've watched the show since the first episode. I've... daydreamed about you a lot."

Kai cocked his head. "Really?"

"Really. So when Felicity suggested applying... it was her idea, but I went along with it. I never dreamed you'd pick me."

"Why not?"

"Because I'm not... Felicity."

Kai frowned. "Who cares about Felicity?"

"I mentioned she's a supermodel, right?"

"She's not you."

Addison's heart skipped a beat. "I'm just a regular person."

"But are you a regular person who thinks she could spend her life with me—here, at Base Camp?" He shifted closer.

Addison nodded.

"Are you sure? There aren't any penthouses here," he cautioned, drawing her into his arms.

"There are tiny houses, though, and they're even cooler." She braced her hands on his chest, loving the feel of his embrace. She'd thought she'd lost this. She could hardly believe she might be wrong.

"What about being an actuary? Could you really leave all that behind?"

She rolled her eyes. "I know what I want to do now. Run the B and B—if the women will let me."

"What about that rich husband Felicity thinks you were hunting for? I'm no millionaire."

"I don't need one. I only need you." She tilted her chin up, and when Kai met her halfway, kissing her so thoroughly Addison became dizzy, she knew she was getting another chance at happiness. She braced her hands on his shoulders, loving the strength of him.

"Are you sure?" Kai asked one more time when they parted again.

"Absolutely. I love you," she said.

"I love you, too."

CHAPTER THIRTEEN

IT WAS LATE that night when Kai finally got to be alone with Addison, and by then he was tight with anticipation and worry. He believed Addison when she said she wanted to stay, but the last twenty-four hours had shaken him more than he cared to admit. He needed to feel her in his arms, to make love to her to prove to himself she was still here.

They'd climbed into his tent together, and he'd freed her from her gown and corset, but instead of stripping off her shift and getting into their sleeping bags, Kai told her there was something he wanted to show her.

They waited, talking quietly, until the camera crews had gone and the camp had settled in for the night before Kai wrapped Addison's warm winter coat around her, lent her some socks, slung the sleeping bags over his shoulder and led her back out into the night.

Their breath puffed white plumes of steam into the cold air, and they hurried toward Pittance Creek, quickly shedding their boots and climbing into the joined sleeping bags when they reached its banks. Kai had positioned them so that they could see an expanse of sky between the trees—an expanse that included a clear sight of a nearly full moon.

Like before, he pulled out two pairs of binoculars and handed one to Addison, then helped her with the settings.

"Take a look."

Addison gasped in surprise when she did. "I can see the mountains and craters on it!"

"Isn't that cool?"

"I never knew you could do this—I thought you needed a telescope."

"A telescope is even better," he admitted.

"But this is great, too." She gazed at it for a long time before turning to him. "Thank you. I could have lived a lifetime in the city and never thought to do this."

"You're welcome." He took her hand and they went back to viewing the moon, until by some unspoken agreement they decided it was time to put the binoculars aside. When Addison turned to snuggle against him, Kai's heart settled into a slow beat. Addison had stayed with him. She'd had the opportunity to live in a penthouse in New York City, and instead, she'd stayed.

"I'm glad you're here," he told her.

"I can't think of anywhere I'd rather be," she admitted. "Kai, you realize you're my dream man, don't you? You're the one who was supposed to be unattainable."

"Is that a bad thing?"

"Well, if this dream of mine can come true, what else might happen?"

"You tell me. What else are you dreaming about?"

She was quiet for a while. "Throwing parties. Lots and lots and lots of parties. Weddings, anniversaries, baby showers, corporate events…"

"I have a feeling that might come true."

"And babies. Someday I want babies."

Kai's arms tightened around her. "I was hoping you'd say that."

"Were you?"

He nodded and found the hem of her shift then tugged it up and over her head. "I think we need to practice."

"That sounds smart." He heard the smile in her voice. "We wouldn't want to mess it up."

"No, we wouldn't." He lifted one of her perfect breasts and bent down to trail a kiss over its softness. Addison sighed and arched closer to him. "Addison," he breathed against her skin. She angled her head to meet his kiss, and they spoke no more for a long time.

ADDISON WELCOMED KAI'S touch like the desert welcomed rain, opening up to his explorations without any hesitation. The way he worshipped her body told her everything she needed to know about their life together. Kai didn't take things for granted, and he cherished the good in the moment. His awareness of the natural world only added to her instinct that he would remain present and thoughtful in their life to come.

Every time they were together, she felt alive, bathed in a sensuous flow of emotions. Kai teased her, awakened her libido and satisfied her in a masterful way. He made her want to stay here with him in these sleeping bags forever, the moon shining down on them, the soft sounds of the forest around them.

But he was quickly coaxing her body to the brink, and Addison dug her fingers into the fabric of the sleeping bags, trying to hold on a little longer, enjoying the sensations he was awakening within her too much to want to let go.

When he pushed inside of her, he completed her universe. He was everything she needed, and every touch of him within her sparked a thousand points of ecstasy. Her need was building with his every thrust, a sensual onslaught of sublime feeling intensifying until she couldn't hold back.

When a final thrust pushed her right over the edge, and she cried out with a sound as wild as any a creature of the woods might make, Kai followed her, bucking into an orgasm that rocked both of them until they finally fell back, spent.

A few minutes later, Kai pulled out, slid to the side and gathered her against him, whispering her name against her hair.

"Can we stay here forever?" she asked him.

His answering chuckle rocked her. "Probably not, but it's tempting."

"I love the moon."

He nodded. "We'll slip out here whenever we can."

"Promise?"

"Promise."

She snuggled against him and pulled him close again.

"HI, I'M KAI Green," Kai said into the camera Byron was holding. "Welcome to *A SEAL's Meals*! Today I'm going to show you how to feed a whole horde of hungry Navy SEALs, among other people, with food you can grow yourself or source locally. Let's get started."

Kai couldn't believe how freeing it was to know he had control over every aspect of his cooking show. He'd picked the recipes, the ingredients, the length of the show, its title—and if he felt like pontificating over the incredible taste of a homegrown heirloom tomato, he could do just that. He would upload it to an online video site. Maybe not the same as being on national television, but like Avery had said, it was only the start.

It had been more satisfying than he could describe to turn down Linkley's offer. He'd expected Renata to be pissed. Instead, she'd agreed to lend him Byron, the cameraman who was always trailing around after Avery.

"Linkley's an ass" was all she said in explanation, but her private smile made him wonder if she bore the man an old grudge she didn't mind seeing answered.

As he mixed, stirred, chopped and cooked, Kai found it wasn't hard at all to keep the patter going. He was talking about all the things he loved to talk about most. And having a ball while he was doing it.

"Let's see what the test group thinks of this freshly grown cauliflower," he said, and the camera pulled back to show the members of *Base Camp* perched around the room. They quickly passed a plate of cauliflower florets around and everyone took one. "We had a minor disaster here at *Base Camp*, and lost most of our vegetable stores. Lucky for us, hardy vegetables like cauliflower can be harvested well into fall, if given a little protection from the elements.

"It's really good, even plain like this," Riley said.

"Way better than store bought," Clay put in.

"Definitely. I'd know; I grew them myself," Samantha said.

"It's great to know where your food comes from," Kai said to the camera. "If you're not a gardener—or a full-on farmer—make friends with someone who is. Purchase a CSA subscription or frequent a farmer's market. There are lots of options these days. And if you can, learn how to grow a variety of foods yourself, so when trouble comes, you've got a backup plan. We had a bumper crop of cabbages, cauliflower and other hardy vegetables, which is going to help us get through what could have been a lean winter. We're also growing more greens and other vegetables in our greenhouses, but we'll talk about that next time."

When the show was done and his friends had clapped and cheered, Avery said, "We'll work on the post-production and get something to you to look at as soon as possible."

"Thank you. I don't know what I would have done without you two." He included the cameraman in his praise.

"You would have filmed it on your phone and it

would have sucked," Avery said with a smile. "Or you would have said yes to Linkley."

"Ugh," Addison put in.

"I like this a lot better. Can't wait to see the final result."

Kai waited for Avery and Byron to hurry off and turned to Addison. "What did you think?"

"I think you're going to be a star."

"Will you still love me when I am?"

"Hell, yeah!"

"ADDISON," NORA CALLED out later when Addison was crossing to her tent to grab her warm jacket. It had grown cold as the afternoon waned. "Can you come up to the manor for a minute? We're having a meeting. Just us women."

"Okay." Addison knew she had nothing to fear, but somehow the request sounded ominous, and as she followed Nora up the path to the large house on top of the hill, she wondered if the rest of the women had something to say about the circumstances under which she'd come here.

Or maybe they wanted to talk about the awkward happenings at the Halloween ball. She'd been happy to hear from Evan that he and her sister had reached Rome safely and were beginning to talk about what had happened that night.

"You'll hear from Felicity soon, I think," Evan had emailed her. "She's very embarrassed, and I've come to understand that leaving New York was a bigger deal than either of us made it out to be. We've held on to the penthouse for now, and we'll take our decisions a bit slower from now on. Your mom's been calling every day, so we've had to set some ground rules. Felicity's going to be the one to call her—once a week at a prearranged time. We've filled in your dad on what's going on, and he's going to try to help persuade your mom that something has to change."

When they reached the manor, Nora went in the back door, which led straight into the kitchen. Addison followed apprehensively and came to an abrupt halt when she saw that someone had laid the table with a linen cloth and the fancy tea service that had come with the place.

"Sit down." Avery gestured to a vacant seat at the end of the table.

"What's all this about?" Addison asked. She looked along the table at the faces smiling back at her.

"Well, aside from the little disturbance your sister caused, the Halloween ball was really lovely," Savannah began.

"And we've had so much extra time these last few weeks to work on our personal projects," Avery continued.

"This last batch of guests was the happiest group we've had," Nora put in.

"You obviously run rings around us as far as organizing and getting things done," Riley said.

"So, this is our way of asking you if you'd like to step into that role for good," Samantha said.

"To become our B and B's director," Avery explained. "We'd pay you a salary to run things, and of course we'd still be involved."

"But we'd give you creative control to come up with special events, develop our wedding business and grow the B and B," Nora said.

"What do you think?" Riley asked.

Addison blinked back tears. "It's more than I could ever have hoped for," she said truthfully. "I've always dreamed of running an event-planning business. I had no idea that when I came here I'd... get an opportunity like this. I love it here," she said. "Just love it here. I don't know what I'd do if I had to leave."

The women pushed back their chairs and came to surround her, each of them offering assurances she'd never have to.

"We love having you here, too," Savannah said.

"We didn't know what we were missing until you arrived," Samantha said, "and I'm not just saying that because you do all my chores at the manor."

With a laugh, Addison allowed them to help her into her seat, pour her some tea and pass her the plate of cookies Avery had baked.

"Yum, these are good," she said.

"Not as good as my films. Just wait until you see the final version of the first episode of *A SEAL's Meals*."

"It's turning out well?" Addison asked.

"It's going to be a hit."

CHAPTER FOURTEEN

A RAGGED CHEER went up from the group when the last roof was finished on the tiny houses. Kai had spent far more time this past week helping to frame in walls than he had cooking—or gardening, although he'd helped with that, too. The interiors were far from finished on the four new dwellings that dotted the hillside, but there'd be enough housing for the couples who married during the winter. Everyone else would have to hunker down the best they could in the bunkhouse.

"Almost makes me want my turn," Curtis joked. Daisy barked.

"Don't you?" Kai asked, angling his head to look at the high clouds sheering over the sky. Snow was coming. Even a California boy like him could smell it in the air.

"You know what they say: twice bitten, shy as fuck." Curtis ruffled his dog's ears.

Kai chuckled, but he felt for the man. "You know what they also say: third time's a charm."

"Hear that?" Curtis yelled to the sky. "Send me a keeper." Daisy barked again, as if in agreement.

Kai wasn't the only one who laughed at that.

"We'll know who goes next in a couple of days," Anders said. "Maybe it'll be me this time."

"Or Walker—seems like it should've been his turn ages ago," Angus said.

Walker only shrugged.

Kai's phone buzzed, and he pulled it out, frowning at the unfamiliar phone number.

"It's Felicity," a female voice said when he accepted the call. "Addison's sister. Do you have a minute to talk?"

"Sure." He took a few steps away from the other men. "What's up?" He knew Addison hadn't talked to her sister since the night of the ball.

"I... need to apologize."

He bit back a sharp retort. She sure as hell did—but not to him. She'd ruined the ball for Addison after all of Addison's hard work.

"I drank too much, and I acted so badly. I don't re-member too much of it, but my husband does, and he's made sure I know every detail."

"Ouch." Sounded like a rotten week in paradise to him.

"Yeah... ouch. How is Addison?"

"Why don't you ask her yourself?" He could tell this was meant to be a warm-up call. Felicity was testing the waters, but that was the coward's way out.

"I will. I know I should be talking to her, not to you,

but... I'm chicken."

"She loves you, you know. You're her sister. She needs you in her life." Kai found himself pacing.

"I know she does, which makes this all worse. I never should have played games with her. I thought I knew better than she did what she needed, but all I ended up doing was breaking her heart. She wanted the penthouse so bad. I should have just given it to her, but I thought she needed more than a place to live—"

"Felicity, you have to have this conversation with Addison."

Felicity drew in a breath. Let it out again. "Yeah. I know. Like I said, I wanted to apologize. I ruined what looked like a lovely night for you two, and I almost ruined everything. It's just... watching the show—I could see her falling in love with Base Camp and with you. I knew she was going to stay in Montana, and I was going to Rome. I felt... like we were never going to see each other again."

Kai stood still. Suddenly, he got it, and despite himself compassion flooded him. He wasn't the only one who feared losing the ones he loved. "You wanted her back in New York. In your penthouse. So even if you were away you could picture where she was and feel close to her."

"Yeah." Felicity was crying. "I'm such a jerk."

"You can come here anytime, you know. Stay at the manor. Dress up like a Jane Austen character. Have a little fun."

"I guess." She was quiet a moment. "Actually, when

you put it like that, it does sound fun."

"It will be. And Addison will love seeing you. Call her, okay?"

"Okay. She's pretty lucky to have found you. I should get some credit for that, right? Maybe enough to make up for what I did at the ball?"

Kai thought about it. "Okay, I can go for that. The slate is clean. Call your sister; she's dying to hear from you."

ADDISON HAD TAKEN charge of gathering up the costumes to return to Alice after the ball. She'd managed to round up all of them except Kai's missing toga. No matter where they looked, she and Kai couldn't find it.

It had been Addison's experience, however, that this was an honorable group of people, and if someone had taken the costume for any reason, she had a hunch they'd give it back, if given the opportunity. She assembled the costumes she had in a large box and left it inside the door of the bunkhouse. As she prepped and cooked with Kai, she tried as best she could to keep her eye on it.

Sure enough, she spotted Avery lingering near it a little before lunchtime. Addison kept watch as Avery carefully slid a rolled-up bundle of white material into the box. Before Avery could slip out of the bunkhouse again, Addison stepped out of the kitchen and shut the door behind her.

"Busted," she said quietly.

"Shit." Avery spun to face her. "Addison—I can explain."

"You don't have to if you don't want to. I'm sure you had your reasons." Although she couldn't guess what they might be. Had Avery needed a toga for some short film she was making? If so, why not simply ask to borrow it?

She remembered Avery hanging around Boone's desk. Remembered Boone asking about a missing paperweight.

Was this the first time Avery had filched something?

Addison took the toga out of the box again, shook it out, refolded it carefully and put it back. "Come here." She led Avery outside to the fire pit and sat down with her on a log. "I need a favor."

"What kind of favor?" Avery eyed her suspiciously.

"The kind of favor you're good at. I need you to steal something for me."

Avery straightened, her face tight with offense, but Addison took her arm and kept her from jumping up. "It's Kai's binder—where he has his recipes and notes. You know what I mean?"

"Why don't you just ask him for it?"

"I want to surprise him. I need to make a digital copy. He has no backup, and he doesn't have a version he can edit, either. I want you to take the binder, scan every page and turn it into a document I can use. Can you do that?"

"Why? He'll be pissed if he catches me, you know."

"I do know that. I also know you're hiding something—something important. Even if I don't know exactly what it is, I can put a stop to it. Do you want me to do that?" Addison held the other woman's gaze until Avery looked away.

"No."

"Do we have a deal?"

"Yeah, we have a deal."

"UP FOR SOME nighttime birdwatching?" Kai asked when they were prepping for dinner.

"Does that mean what I think it means?" Addison asked, stopping midway through slicing one of the last onions. She'd been out in the greenhouses with Kai earlier that day and had admired the new lettuces that were growing well. There were green onions poking their heads up and even potato plants. They hadn't solved their food problem completely, but there was hope, as Kai had told her.

"That means exactly what you think it means," Kai said, brushing a kiss over her cheek as he passed to fetch something else from the refrigerator.

There weren't any camera crews in the room today. As soon as they stepped out of the kitchen, however, they'd be trailed all day, which is why a nighttime excursion was his only chance of proposing to Addison alone. He'd done it once already, but he wanted to do it again. With a ring, this time. He wanted proof of her pledge on her finger—not because he didn't believe her, but because he wanted to be reminded every time she was nearby that he was going to get to be with her for the rest of his life.

Besides, making love to Addison under a canopy of stars was one of his favorite things to do.

First, however, he needed a ring. He waited until they'd served lunch and Addison had gone off with the other women to the manor to prepare for their next round of guests.

Curtis met him in the door to the kitchen. "Boone sent me," he said. "Wants to know if we're having a wedding this weekend?" He must have left his dog with someone else; there was no sign of Daisy.

"One way or the other," Kai said. "I'm off to buy a ring right now."

"I'll come with you," Curtis said.

"Sure. I could use the moral support."

Curtis was too quiet on the ride into town to offer much support, however, and Kai wondered what was on the man's mind. He expected him to head off on an errand of his own when he parked on the street near Thayer's, the sole jewelry store in town, but Curtis stuck close, even when they entered the store.

As Kai searched for an engagement ring to give to Addison when he proposed, Curtis perused the trays of rings, too. It took a long time for Kai to settle on a gold ring with a sweep of diamonds like a wave crashing against the shore. It was elegant, and he thought it suited Addison. He turned to show it to Curtis and found the man holding a ring of his own.

"Have you been seeing someone?" Kai asked him, intrigued. Since Harris had stolen the bride Boone had chosen for Curtis, the man had seemed far too withdrawn from the world to get up to much of anything. Now Kai wondered if Curtis had fooled them all.

"Nope." Curtis shook his head. "But I thought about our talk the other day, and I've decided I'm going to. I'm not going to wait to draw a straw or for someone else to pick me a bride. I'm here at Base Camp. I've pledged to get married. I'm going to find my own woman. And this is the ring I'll give her." He held up a ring Kai hadn't seen—a large oblong diamond surrounded by smaller ones set in a platinum band.

"That's a hell of a ring."

"My future wife deserves it. I won't pick a woman who doesn't."

Curtis was a man on a mission. Kai was impressed.

"You two gentlemen finding everything okay?" A petite woman with dark hair came to help them.

"I'd like to buy this ring," Kai said and handed the pretty bit of jewelry to the clerk. "I'm Kai Green. From Base Camp."

"I recognized you. I'm Rose Johnson. Nice to meet you." She held the ring in the palm of her hand, and her gaze grew distant for a moment. When she focused on him again, she smiled. "You and your fiancée are going to be very happy together."

"I sure hope so."

They completed the transaction, and Rose handed him the ring in a small velvet-covered box. "Good luck."

"Thanks."

"I want to buy a ring, too," Curtis declared. "This one."

"Oh—I didn't realize you were looking, too. Is it going to be a double wedding?" Rose asked with a smile.

"I'm definitely looking." Curtis ignored her question and handed it over, and Rose repeated her earlier move, curling her fingers over it, her gaze going slack. She frowned suddenly. Her brows furrowed.

She bit her lip. "Um..." She looked like she would hand it back to him before she caught herself, straightened her shoulders, tightened her grip on the ring and closed her eyes.

Kai and Curtis exchanged a look. Curtis raised an eyebrow. Kai shrugged.

Rose opened her eyes, a smile playing around her lips. "You... have an interesting journey ahead of you," she told Curtis as she moved back to the counter and began to ring him up. "The woman who fits this ring is going to lead you on a merry chase."

"But there is a woman out there for me?" Curtis asked, as if she might know the answer. Kai wondered if she did; there was something fey about Rose.

She stopped, her hands hovering over the keys of the cash register. "Of course there's a woman for you."

Curtis just nodded, but Kai saw a muscle working in his friend's jaw.

Curtis had needed to hear that.

Kai was glad he had.

ADDISON AND KAI slipped out of the tent long past midnight and tiptoed through the encampment and down the path toward Pittance Creek. Like last time, she was dressed only in her shift and coat, and tonight was so cold she shivered as they hurried to the creek. On its banks, Kai made a bed of four sleeping bags—they'd each been issued a second one because of the plunging temperatures—and they snuggled together under their covers, their heads resting on the pillow Addison had brought.

Soon she was warm enough to shed her spencer, and it wasn't long before both of them had shucked off the rest of their clothing. Pressed against Kai's hard body, Addison's pulse accelerated knowing soon they'd be together. Nothing could compare to the spectacular beauty of this natural setting. It was so quiet she felt like she and Kai were the only ones in the world.

"It must have been like this in the old days," she said.

"Can you imagine prehistoric times? Only a few hundred thousand people spread across all of Europe," he said. "So much space. The world must have felt so big."

She nodded and rested her head on Kai's chest, hearing his heartbeat. It was all such a mystery—the past, the present.

The future.

"Do you think we'll ever find out who stole our food?" she asked him.

"Probably not. I have a feeling Montague's involved,

though."

"That makes sense." She thought of Avery stealing Kai's costume. And Boone's paperweight. She'd wondered briefly if her friend could be behind the theft of the food, too, but she'd decided it was unlikely. Kai had told her the break-in had occurred during Harris and Sam's wedding, and some subtle questioning proved Avery hadn't left the celebration. Addison decided to keep Avery's mischief to herself—for now. Taking the costume hadn't hurt anyone—except Addison's own pride when she'd mistakenly kissed Evan. Taking their food would put everyone at risk. Avery wouldn't do that.

"Addison." Kai shifted and pulled something out of the depths of the sleeping bag. A little box.

Addison stilled, her heart in her mouth, and forgot all about Avery.

"I know I asked you this before, but I want to ask you one more time. I want to do this right. You know now what my life is about. You know Base Camp, the people here, the work—the possibility we could lose it all. You know, too, how much I love you. How much I'd do to keep you happy. So, Addison—" He sat up and opened the box, exposing a beautiful ring that made Addison bite her lip and scramble up to sit, too. "Will you make me the happiest man on earth and be my wife?"

"Yes." Addison blinked back tears as he slid the ring on her finger. It glittered there, promising a new life. An exciting, invigorating, incredible life with the man she loved. "Yes," she said again. "Yes, yes, yes."

Kai leaned in and kissed her, and Addison flung her arms around his neck.

"Do you want to—"

"Make love? Yes," she said again. "What's taking you so long?"

"Didn't realize you were in such a hurry."

As they snuggled back down into their sleeping bags, the stars and moon glittering overhead, Addison gave herself up to a world of pleasure with the man she loved.

CHAPTER FIFTEEN

E ARLY ON HER wedding day, Addison slipped into the bunkhouse.

"Hey, I'm not supposed to see you until we meet at the altar, right?" Kai tried to cover his eyes with his hands, only half-serious; he'd spent last night with her, and they'd only separated a half hour ago.

"You're not supposed to see me in my dress. I'm still in my street clothes." She indicated her Regency gown. "I've got something for you. A surprise."

"I've got something for you, too. I planned to give it to you later tonight, though." The beautiful necklace and bracelet set Rose had helped him pick out when he'd gone back to Thayer's was sitting in his tent.

"I'll look forward to it," she told him and handed him a flat, heavy package.

Kai made short work of opening it; they didn't have much time before they needed to help with preparations for the wedding.

"A tablet. Cool." He turned it over, wondering if she'd had something in mind when she chose it.

"Turn it on." Addison showed him and tapped it a few times until a document came up. "Here's the real present."

Kai took the tablet back and scanned the heading of the document. *"A SEAL's Meals: Recipes and Tips for Feeding Hungry Warriors."* He scrolled down the page. "What is—how did you—it's my book!"

"Exactly; it's your book. Kai, you already wrote one—you just need to get it in order. All we did was scan your notebook and get the words into text you can manipulate. All your illustrations are in there, too. This will make it easy for you to play with the information and get it ready to publish—if you want to."

"Hell, yeah, I want to. I just couldn't figure out how to get past the mess in my notebook."

"There's more," Addison said. She took the tablet back, tapped a few more buttons and handed it to him.

"You made a website?"

"Avery did. It's somewhere to sell the book and get your message across. Avery says you need multiple platforms for your brand. Whatever that means," she added with a lift of her shoulder. "I guess I need to learn so I can market our B and B better. When I do, I'll pass it on."

"How'd you do this? I use that notebook every day. It was never missing."

"That I'll never tell," she said and kissed him. "Now I've got to run. See you at the altar."

He pulled her in for a more satisfying kiss. "Can't wait."

Addison slipped away, and twenty minutes later, Kai met his parents, brother and sisters and nephews and niece on the way to the manor.

"Kai!" Grace said, bounding up to him, tugging a man along with her. It had to be her fiancé. "Kai, this is Tom Bixby. Tom, this is my brother."

Kai shook hands with Tom, a square-jawed, sensible-looking man in his late thirties who Kai immediately liked. He looked like he could handle what life threw at him. Like he'd be a good partner for Kai's sister. His hair was short, his build stocky. He walked like a policeman, Kai thought, biting back a grin.

"You two had better be friends," Grace warned them.

"We will be," Kai told her.

"I don't think we have a choice," Tom said to him. "Your sister doesn't put up with much insubordination."

"Good." Grace looked wonderful. Happy, Kai thought. "Looking forward to your wedding."

"June eighth," Grace said. "You'll have to come to California, though."

"Kai, I'm so proud of you," Wanda interrupted, throwing her arms around him as soon as she reached him.

"What happened to 'this is all a crazy mistake—don't marry a stranger'?" Kai asked her.

"I've been watching the show, and I like Addison. She's going to be good for you; she's got a real head on her shoulders."

Kai didn't protest that he had a good head on his shoulders, too. He knew what his mother meant to say; she was happy for him.

He was happy, too.

Soon he was swarmed with Celia's kids, and he reveled in boisterous love of his extended family. It meant a lot to him that they'd all showed up when his courtship and marriage were so unusual. The Ledbetters were all about family, though. Kai once again offered a prayer of thanks to whoever was listening for bringing him and his sister to such a solid, stable family after the chaos of their earliest years. He sent another prayer of hope that his biological mom had found some kind of peace and happiness, too.

He left his family in Riley's capable hands at the manor's front door, passed Maud and James busy overseeing an army of helpers set up the folding chairs in rows in the ballroom and continued up the stairs to the second floor. He and the rest of the men of Base Camp had been assigned to a guest bedroom for last-minute fittings of the Revolutionary War–era uniforms it had become the custom for them to don on wedding days. The uniforms matched the Regency dresses of the women, and Kai didn't mind; it made the women happy.

Alice, who kept a store of the costumes for the reenactments done each year in Chance Creek, had brought over the ones they used and was giving everyone a once-over to make sure they still fit. As groom, his uniform was given several embellishments for the day. Once he'd changed, Alice came to make sure he looked dashing enough to stand up with Addison.

"Here comes the best part," she said gaily when the door opened and Walker and Boone stepped in, followed by a camera crew.

Kai knew what she meant. Each time one of them married, the remaining single men drew straws to see who was next. He remembered his own shock at pulling the short straw. At the time he'd been so freaked out he hadn't slept for days.

Now he couldn't remember what all the fuss had been about.

"Line up," Boone said. "Angus, Anders, Curtis, Greg and Walker, that means you. Five of us down and five left to go. Let's see who's the next victim."

Anders seemed ready to choose. Greg not so much, and Angus not at all if his lowered brow and pursed lips were any indication. Walker was as stoic as ever.

But before any of them could lean forward to draw a straw, Curtis elbowed past the rest, grabbed all the straws out of Walker's fist and picked out the short one.

"There. I'm going next. Did you get that?" He waved the short straw in front of the closest camera. "Me. I'm the next victim." He stalked out of the room.

"Well, I guess that's that," Boone said slowly.

"Huh. Another forty days' reprieve," Anders said, a grin tugging at his mouth.

"Thank God," Angus said darkly.

"HEY, KIDDO," ADDISON'S father said, knocking on the doorframe. "Is it okay for me to come in?"

"Dad! You made it!" Addison hopped down off the little stool she'd been standing on while Alice made last-minute alterations. The other women of Base Camp had been flowing in and out of the guest room she'd been assigned all morning, oohing and aahing over the beautiful dress Alice had made for her and helping out however they could.

Her father caught her in a bear hug. Behind him, she spied her mother, hanging back as if unsure of her welcome.

"Mom!" Addison moved to give her a hug, too. "I'm so glad you're here."

"Wouldn't miss it for the world," her father said. Her mother was too busy looking around, taking in the old-fashioned loveliness of the bedroom. "I met the groom downstairs," he added. "Fine, upstanding man. I think you picked a good one. Although… you two are moving pretty fast, huh?"

"It's the show," she explained. "We don't have much choice."

"Well, you look beautiful, of course," her father told her. "Marjorie, doesn't she look beautiful?"

Again, her mother hesitated. "Yes," she said. "You look very beautiful."

"I'm going to make sure your mother finds her seat downstairs," her father said. "Then I'll be back to walk you down the aisle." They left again without further ado.

"They seem nice," Alice said.

"My mom's being weird," Addison said.

"She's minding her Ps and Qs, I'd say," Alice remarked.

When Addison's father returned, he took her aside and confirmed that. "We went to a counselor," he said. "Felicity decamping to Europe brought home a few things."

"You think Mom will be okay?"

"Sure, I do," he said heartily. "She'll find another project sooner or later. Her own, I hope."

Addison hoped so, too.

"You sure you're ready for this?" he asked as they prepared to go downstairs.

"Absolutely. I'm happier than I've ever been in my life."

"I'm glad to hear that. I wish Felicity was here to see you."

"I know. But I'm glad she's getting a chance to start over, too."

"Wise girl. I think you're going to make Kai a very happy man."

"I'm going to try."

KAI HELD HIS breath when Addison stepped down the grand staircase, her arm linked with her father's, and entered the ballroom, where he waited at a temporary altar next to Curtis and Angus. Reverend Halpern stood serenely close by.

He'd thought his world had ended when he drew the short straw forty days ago, but now he knew fate was on his side. He was sure he'd make a good life with Addison. Both of them would be busy, creative, challenged by their work, soothed by each other's presence.

He wanted to be the best husband to her he could. The best father to the children they'd have someday.

They'd have a community that was as tight, warm and supportive as they could wish for. Worthy work, and he'd get the chance to spread the word about the subject he was most passionate about.

But most of all he was thankful fate had provided Addison.

He couldn't remember ever having someone in his life he could talk to the way he talked to her. Nor could he remember being as on fire for any woman he'd known before. Addison was the perfect combination. Love wrapped up in intelligence. Sex wrapped up in a best friend. A man couldn't ask for more.

As she came to stand beside him, he took her hand, looked into her eyes and bent to kiss her, needing to let her know he hadn't changed his mind and never would.

"A-hem," Reverend Halpern said. A comfortable, middle-aged minister, he was a man whose sense of humor—and common sense—Kai had appreciated in the days leading up to the wedding. "Let's get through the ceremony first." He winked to let them know he was kidding.

Halpern opened his mouth to begin, and Addison went up on tiptoe and kissed the underside of Kai's chin.

When Halpern cleared his throat again, both of them laughed.

"We're ready," Kai said.

"Dearly Beloved," Halpern said quickly, and the

ceremony began.

ADDISON THOUGHT SHE'D never been happier. So much of her life had improved in the last few weeks, things she hadn't dreamed she could change. She was in love, for one thing—deeply, wildly, head over heels in love with a man she found fascinating and fun.

She'd found a community, for another thing. Fifteen people and counting who were all as deeply dedicated to building something together as she was.

She'd found a calling, too. A way to help people, brighten people's lives, facilitate their vacations from their regular existence and tug at their dreams to widen their horizons. She'd freed her new friends from some of the work that wasn't as fun for them so they could pursue their true desires.

She'd found a way back to her family, as well. She had always loved her parents and sister, and they'd always loved her, but she thought now they were on the road to becoming close in a far healthier way.

Had ever a bride entered her new life with so much happiness? Addison didn't think that was possible. When Kai slid her wedding band on her finger, it felt like a promise fulfilled. She was so happy to share her life with him. So excited to begin it together.

"You may now kiss the bride," Reverend Halpern intoned.

"Ready for the rest of our lives?" Kai asked her, taking her into his arms.

"Yes!"

To find out more about Harris, Samantha, Boone, Riley, Clay, Jericho, Walker and the other inhabitants of Westfield, look for *A SEAL's Resolve*, Volume 6 in the *SEALs of Chance Creek* series.

Be the first to know about Cora Seton's new releases! Sign up for her newsletter here!

www.coraseton.com/sign-up-for-my-newsletter

Other books in the SEALs of Chance Creek Series:

A SEAL's Oath

A SEAL's Vow

A SEAL's Pledge

A SEAL's Consent

A SEAL's Resolve

A SEAL's Devotion

A SEAL's Desire

A SEAL's Struggle

A SEAL's Triumph

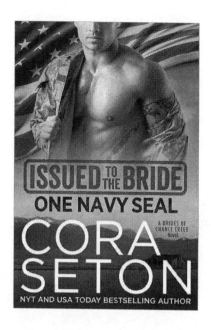

Read on for an excerpt of
Issued to the Bride One Navy SEAL.

Four months ago

ON THE FIRST of February, General Augustus Reed entered his office at USSOCOM at MacDill Air Force Base in Tampa, Florida, placed his battered leather briefcase on the floor, sat down at his wide, wooden desk and pulled a sealed envelope from a drawer. It bore the date written in his wife's beautiful script, and the General ran his thumb over the words before turning it over and opening the flap.

He pulled out a single page and began to read.

Dear Augustus,

It's time to think of our daughters' future, beginning with Cass.

The General nodded. Spot on, as usual; he'd been thinking about Cass a lot these days. Thinking about all the girls. They'd run yet another of his overseers off Two Willows, his wife's Montana ranch, several months ago, and he'd been forced to replace him with a man he didn't know. There was a long-standing feud between him and the girls over who should run the place, and the truth was, they were wearing him down. Ten overseers in eleven years; that had to be some kind of a record, and no ranch could function well under those circumstances. Still, he'd be damned if he was going to put a passel of rebellious daughters in charge, even if they were adults now. It took a man's steady hand to run such a large spread.

Unfortunately, it was beginning to come clear that Bob Finchley didn't possess that steady hand. Winter in Chance Creek was always a tricky time, but in the months since Finchley had taken the helm, they'd lost far too many cattle. The General's spies in the area reported the ranch was looking run-down, and his daughters hadn't been seen much in town. The worst were the rumors about Cass and Finchley—that they were dating. The General didn't like that at all—not if the man couldn't run the ranch competently—and he'd asked for confirmation, but so far it hadn't come. Finchley always had a rational explanation for the loss of cattle, and he never said a word about Cass, but the General knew something wasn't right and he was already looking for the man's replacement.

Our daughter runs a tight ship, and I'm sure she's been invaluable on the ranch.

He had to admit what Amelia wrote was true. Cass was an organizational wizard. She kept her sisters, the house and the family accounts in line, and not for the first time he wondered if he should have encouraged Cass to join the Army back when she had expressed interest. She'd mentioned the possibility once or twice as a teenager, but he'd discouraged her. Not that he didn't think she'd make a good soldier; she'd have made a fine one. It was the thought of his five daughters scattered to the wind that had guided his hand. He couldn't stomach that. He needed his family in one place, and he'd done what it took to keep her home. That wasn't much: a suggestion her sisters needed her to watch over them until they were of age, a mention of tasks undone on the ranch, a hint she and the others would inherit one day and shouldn't she watch over her inheritance? It had done the trick.

Maybe he'd been wrong.

But if Cass had gone, wouldn't the rest of them have followed her?

He'd been able to stop sending guardians for the girls when Cass turned twenty-one five years ago, much to everyone's relief. His daughters had liked those about as little as they liked the overseers. He'd hoped when he dispensed of the guardians, the girls would feel they had enough independence, but that wasn't the case; they still wanted control of the ranch.

Cass is a loving soul with a heart as big as Montana, but she's cautious, too. I'll wager she's beginning to think there isn't a man alive she can trust with it.

The General sighed. His girls hadn't confided in him in years—especially about matters of the heart—something he was glad Amelia couldn't know. The truth was his daughters had spent far too much time as teenagers hatching plots to cast off guardians and overseers to have much of a social life. They'd been obsessed with being independent, and there were stretches of time when they'd managed it—and managed to run the show with no one the wiser for months. In order to pull that off, they'd kept to themselves as much as possible. He'd only recently begun to hear rumblings about men and boyfriends. Unfortunately, none of the girls were picking hardworking men who might make a future at Two Willows; they were picking flashy, fly-by-night troublemakers.

Like Bob Finchley.

He couldn't understand it. He wanted that man out of there. Now. Trouble was, when your daughters ran off so many overseers it made it hard to get a new one to sign on. He had yet to find a suitable replacement.

Without a career off the ranch, Cass won't get out much. She might not ever meet the man who's right for her. I want you to step in. Send her a man, Augustus. A good man.

A good man. Those weren't easy to come by in this world. The right man for Cass would need to be strong to hold his own in a relationship with her. He'd need to be fair and true, or he wouldn't be worthy of her. He'd need some experience ranching.

A lot of experience ranching.

The General stopped to ponder that. He'd read something recently about a man with a lot of experience ranching. A good man who'd gotten into a spot of trouble. He remembered thinking he ought to get a second chance—with a stern warning not to screw up again. A Navy SEAL, wasn't it? He'd look up the document when he was done.

He returned to the letter.

> *Now here's the hard part, darling. You can't order him to marry Cass any more than you can order Cass to marry him. You're a cunning old codger when you want to be, and it'll take all your deviousness to pull this off. Set the stage. Introduce the players.*
>
> *Let fate do the rest.*
>
> *I love you and I always will,*
> *Amelia*

Set the stage. Introduce the players.

The General read through the letter a second time, folded it carefully, slid it back into the envelope and added it to the stack in his deep, right-hand bottom drawer. He steepled his hands and considered his options. Amelia was right; he needed to do something to make sure his daughters married well. But they'd rebelled against him for years, so he couldn't simply assign them husbands, as much as he'd like to. They'd never allow the interference.

But if he made them think they'd chosen the right men themselves...

He nodded. That was the way to go about it.

In fact...

The General chuckled. Sometime in the next six months, his daughters would stage another rebellion and evict Bob Finchley from the ranch. He could just about guarantee it, even if Cass was currently dating the man. Sooner or later he'd go too far trying to boss them around, and Cass and the others would flip their lids.

When they did, he'd be ready for them with a re-placement they'd never be able to shake. One trained to combat enemy forces by good ol' Uncle Sam himself. A soldier in the Special Forces might do it. Or maybe even a Navy SEAL...

This wasn't the work of a moment, though. He'd need time to put the players in place. Cass wasn't the only one who'd need a man—a good man—to share her life.

Five daughters.

Five husbands.

Amelia would approve.

The General opened the bottom left-hand drawer of his desk, and mentally counted the remaining envelopes that sat unopened in another stack, all dated in his wife's beautiful script. Ten years ago, after Amelia passed away, Cass had forwarded him a plain brown box filled with envelopes she'd received from the family lawyer. The stack in this drawer had dwindled compared to the opened ones in the other drawer.

What on earth would he do when there were none left?

End of Excerpt

The Cowboys of Chance Creek Series:

The Cowboy Inherits a Bride (Volume 0)
The Cowboy's E-Mail Order Bride (Volume 1)
The Cowboy Wins a Bride (Volume 2)
The Cowboy Imports a Bride (Volume 3)
The Cowgirl Ropes a Billionaire (Volume 4)
The Sheriff Catches a Bride (Volume 5)
The Cowboy Lassos a Bride (Volume 6)
The Cowboy Rescues a Bride (Volume 7)
The Cowboy Earns a Bride (Volume 8)
The Cowboy's Christmas Bride (Volume 9)

The Heroes of Chance Creek Series:

The Navy SEAL's E-Mail Order Bride (Volume 1)
The Soldier's E-Mail Order Bride (Volume 2)
The Marine's E-Mail Order Bride (Volume 3)
The Navy SEAL's Christmas Bride (Volume 4)
The Airman's E-Mail Order Bride (Volume 5)

The SEALs of Chance Creek Series:

A SEAL's Oath

A SEAL's Vow

A SEAL's Pledge

A SEAL's Consent

A SEAL's Purpose

A SEAL's Resolve

A SEAL's Devotion

A SEAL's Desire

A SEAL's Struggle

A SEAL's Triumph

The Brides of Chance Creek Series:

Issued to the Bride One Navy SEAL

Issued to the Bride One Airman

Issued to the Bride One Sniper

Issued to the Bride One Marine

Issued to the Bride One Soldier

The Turners v. Coopers Series:

The Cowboy's Secret Bride (Volume 1)

The Cowboy's Outlaw Bride (Volume 2)

The Cowboy's Hidden Bride (Volume 3)

The Cowboy's Stolen Bride (Volume 4)

The Cowboy's Forbidden Bride (Volume 5)

About the Author

NYT and USA Today bestselling author Cora Seton loves cowboys, hiking, gardening, bike-riding, and lazing around with a good book. Mother of four, wife to a computer programmer/backyard farmer, she recently moved to Victoria and looks forward to a brand new chapter in her life. Like the characters in her Chance Creek series, Cora enjoys old-fashioned pursuits and modern technology, spending mornings in her garden, and afternoons writing the latest Chance Creek romance novel. Visit **www.coraseton.com** to read about new releases, contests and other cool events!

Blog:

www.coraseton.com

Facebook:

www.facebook.com/coraseton

Twitter:

www.twitter.com/coraseton

Newsletter:

www.coraseton.com/sign-up-for-my-newsletter

Made in the USA
Lexington, KY
15 March 2018